The Kaleidoscope

Adrian Mendoza

Copyright © 2014 Adrian Mendoza

All rights reserved.

ISBN: 150520358
ISBN-13: 978-1505209358

FOR TING
AND LULU

CONTENTS

	Acknowledgments	i
1	Annihilation	1
2	Messiah's Complex	14
3	True Believer	25
4	The Divide	32
5	Order Up	48
6	Human Error	56
7	Of Two Minds	66
8	Projections	76
9	Measured Variance	88
10	The Neglected	100
11	The Reckoning	109

12	A Spectacle	120
13	Close Ranks	132
14	Hemorrhaging	144
15	Toast of the Town	156
16	Epilogue	167

THE KALEIDOSCOPE

ACKNOWLEDGMENTS

First and foremost I thank my wife, Teresa. Her unwavering support and dedication allowed me to write when possible.

I would like to thank: the Mendoza, Vasquez, Lemus, Salas, Otanez, Valdivia, and Gonzalez families in San Diego and Mexico; the Catudan, Panma, Pambid, and Gonzales families throughout Northern California and the Philippines.

1 ANNIHILATION

In the near future.

Alec Helena's companies had afforded him the luxury of being one of the few Elites in a world that operated within an alternate reality. At the level of the Elites most everything operated with the most advanced automation. The few with access to such technology were all too familiar with Alec's precise manner. He had proved genial amongst the peers he had burned on his rise to power. Yet, there remained a magnetic sharpness to him.

Helena's olive skin beamed against the crisp white collar of his charcoal colored designer suit. He ignored his reflection wherever present except for the black wells he had for eyes, whose reflective void pierced and numbed his concentration. Mechanized pangs of regret sprawled across this dark horizon. He could see the masses crawling in desperation for his slightest recognition. Resentment arose as the city lights illuminated the gap between himself and the rest of society. With little effort, his infinite gaze adjusted to the sanctuary of indifference surrounding him. Lifelong advice surfaced.

"Empathy is for those foolish enough to believe they are not animals."

For a moment the contrast of office lighting and his frame's edge upon the window caught his attention. He imagined himself a vessel of devoured competitors whose sacrifices had granted him dominion over the heap of city below.

The Helena Building towered over the Manhattan skyline. As *the* global economic center, it never lacked for traffic. Lifetimes were dedicated to gaining entrance to its daily grind.

As a torrential midnight neared, a forced acquisition was to occur. Alec's bio-engineering companies were on the verge of becoming the first global monopoly over the last of the leading robotics manufacturers. He already owned the most lucrative human gene and robotics patents so his focus was on wrangling in the stragglers.

The competing Chinese corporations had self-imploded due to a series of people's revolutions. Over the same period specialized German tech companies had merged with the Helena Corporation. The systems of global regulatory banking had met their inevitable western unification.

Alec was gifted in a great many of things, but most of all, in recognizing opportunity. From major acquisitions, he chose twelve particular executives to occupy his board of directors. The twelve men and women were present and accounted for, and waited in the boardroom next door to Alec's office.

The impending acquisition would be that of the last of the unified Chinese tech firms. It could have been as easily completed without a single representative present - a few hand swipes of authorization from the other side of the globe would have sufficed. Just as each of his board members once had, the latest employee representatives would partake in the demeaning process of a physical signature.

The horrendous rainstorm made the night especially rewarding. The building's sole helicopter pad was on reserve for Alec, so every representative attending arrived in the most basic of Self-Driven Vehicle (SDV) sedans which were forced to double-park far down and across the street. After facing the elements, the humiliation continued as each representative had their person searched upon arrival by building security. They were then ordered to remain in the lobby until summoned. Then, with only five dreadful minutes remaining until their midnight appointment, a call arrived which sent them scurrying into the elevators. The already beleaguered representatives were forced to run towards the boardroom with only automated executive assistants pointing the way. The board made no attempt to welcome their anxious guests.

Alec sat with his eyes closed at the head of the boardroom dozing. No one dared wake him as the guests moved along the back wall. The young Chinese executives looked at the ceiling or along the walls, feeling unnaturally compressed as they waited within the spacious boardroom. When Alec finally opened his eyes, he smiled. With his attention focused on a pen at the opposite end of the table he gestured with his hand for the representatives to form a line.

Paper contracts were signed; attempted handshakes were rejected. The group slithered away thanking the board members and Alec for their time. The signing was but a formality of recognition. Alec had learned long ago that such order benefited the whole.

When the last of the acquired employees had left the property appropriately uncertain of their future, it was time for the board to enjoy themselves. The party remained in full swing in the boardroom until a red light flashed on and off through one of the windows. It was Alec's robotic executive assistant. It was flashing a personal emergency contact that then spread out to the network of executive assistants throughout the floor. Because Alec had proven very adept at keeping free from entanglements, the emergency line had never before rung.

Alec assumed there must have been a glitch in the programming. Such glitches were exactly why he kept human employees in positions he considered vital. With a few of the more persistent brownnosers in tow, he walked towards the closest executive assistant.

Alec's network of faceless, female voiced, advanced robots operated the day-to-day affairs of the office. Their upper torsos, heads, and arms gleamed with a gun metal finish. They were faceless, legless, and nameless; they never left their station.

It was not that it was illegal to have a humanoid robot. Such laws had faded some years ago due to strong demand. But Alec preferred dealing with traditional robots that lacked any superficial qualities. He had a personal disdain for mechanized mannequins that fostered a perceived sense of control. Robots were appliances that functioned according to design, and nothing more. When he approached, the robot assistant spoke: "Sir, you received an incoming message about your son."

Taken aback by such an unexpected announcement, he demanded: "What did you say?"

The robot moved its head a few degrees to the right and back again, only to reword the message: "Sir, an incoming message about your son."

Alec's entourage of brownnosers stared at the robot. Then, as rational thinking kicked in, they assumed something must have gone wrong with the old model. In all the articles and conversations they could recall, there had never been any mention of Mr. Helena having any family beyond his parents: his father had died long ago; his mother had passed away no more than a decade ago.

Alec grasped his chin and became infuriated with the board members in tow and the onlookers behind them. He turned to them. "Get out of my face ... now!"

Without hesitation, they rushed back to the boardroom and closed the glass doors behind them.

A few veteran employees recalled rumors of Alec having married and an overdose or some other pitiful death. Never having had any merit, the rumors were considered nothing more than petty gossip. With Alec's strong connections to the media, it was not surprising that most every rumor was eventually reduced to mere gossip. With such influence he had long ago created his chosen – that of a lone trailblazer. Alec's debonair demeanor wore off completely.

"Explain yourself robot!"

"Sir, the police ended their call after placed on hold per your request during all: meetings, acquisitions, lawsuits… "

In an attempt to compose himself, he interrupted: "Yes! And as for the message?"

The arrival of another message caused the executive assistant to deliver pause.

"Sir, incoming call."

Alec, who was aware of his audience, attempted to play down the incoming call: "Here we go, put it through."

A small New York City Police Department logo flashed across the robot's face. The identification badge that followed was of an overworked detective.

"Good morning Mr. Helena, this is Detective Martinez. We need for you to come to the address that I'm sending to you as soon as possible."

Alec turned towards the conference room. With a swipe of his hand, the room's windows frosted and became soundproof. Alec leaned over the counter and spoke into the glossy faceplate so that the detective could hear him loud and clear: "What's this about? Know that both you and your direct superior will be on notice!"

He reached out to mute the call by air tapping the robot's chin. With abundant frustration he asked the robot: "Why did you put this call through?"

Det. Martinez overrode the mute. "Sir, you need to come down here as soon as possible, it's your son."

Alec leaned in. "Whatever this *person* did or did not do, I'll have someone take care of it. There are protocols for this sort of matter Detective... Martinez - badge number... 1016."

Alec's reaction was a matter of containment. As he stepped away, the detective, irritated by the attempted dismissal, blurted: "Sir, we only need for you to identify the body. Then you can do as you please. This is a courtesy call per our standard operating procedures on all Elites and or their families and associates. We hope to see you soon. Good day."

Before the call ended, Alec overheard some of the detective's unofficial griping. "These rich types are such... "

The color drained from Alec's face. All he could do was to gaze into the chrome abyss of the executive assistant that offered nothing more than a warped reflection. An address scrolled across the faceplate and the robot spoke: "Sir, your helicopter is ready. Do you have instructions for the board?"

He straightened his shoulders before un-frosting the boardroom windows. Whatever conversations the occupants were having immediately ceased. Alec issued this warning to the robotic assistant: "My instructions are for them to get out of my building. My advice is, if they even think about mentioning anything of my personal life... I will end them."

As the message was relayed, the boardroom fell into a flurried motion. Exiting the building was the only objective.

While crossing over railings to the brick-shaped helicopter, the helipad robot handed Alec a chrome handled umbrella. The amber lighting slits from the umbrella's stem base reflected the full downpour of rain. As Alec approached, the tucked away helicopter rotors began to spread out. Once aboard, Alec attempted to collect his thoughts. He slid the umbrella into the door pocket, put on his headset and removed a wand scroll from his seat armrest. Its sheet of transparent plastic became rigid and illuminated at his touch as he pulled it across his lap. He began to track the helicopter's relative position as its vertical thrust trailed into the darkened sky.

The target destination was highlighting an area due south of the Bronx. A host of relevant articles organized themselves into virtual bundles upon the screen. All the headings involved crime. A live satellite image appeared after a visual acknowledgment. It was the definitive dead end of a neighborhood. The narrow walkways and debris filled alleys screamed criminal activity. Vacant lots opened to gutted buildings. He crimped the edges of the scroll and thought.

"They must have called to report the body hours ago. What was I doing during that time?"

Alec released the scroll and allowed it to roll back up as it slid off of his lap. It flickered off as it settled along his shoe. Alec pulled his headset off. He muttered choice words into his fist before concluding: "It can't be him - it's probably some junkie. Well, wait a minute. The police do have some rather sophisticated identification equipment."

He paused at the thought of denying the body's actual identity. The pilot knocked on the window as he tapped on his headset. Alec slipped his headset back on. The pilot said: "Sir, we're going to have to land here. The clearing below is the closest we can get. There's no other level ground."

Mud and debris were cast about as the helicopter landed near the mouth of a dark and narrow alley.

On the descent, Alec squinted through his rain spattered windows. Upon landing, the door to the helicopter opened and the storm outside came roaring in. The rotors were quieting down but the rain was pouring so hard it near masked the smell of concrete muck. In the distance he saw what he could only assume were two detectives standing beneath a stubborn awning. Across from them were two police officers armed with department issued assault rifles.

Alec expected at least one of the detectives to walk over and guide him. Neither of the detectives budged an inch. The helicopter's pilot shifted his weight uneasily at the awkward standoff. Alec looked on in disbelief.

Grudgingly exiting the helicopter, Alec noticed the countless homeless people lining every stretch of the adjacent buildings. Alec took a deep breath from the interior of the helicopter as he reached back in to retrieve the umbrella from the door.

Alec Helena walked upstream a jigsaw of protruding concrete to his destination. Halfway, one detective too tall for his own coat, disappeared down the alley. Detective Martinez remained. He was an anemic specter of a man, wearing an old fashioned trench coat and an inappropriate grin. Alec was careful in maneuvering every mud splattered step remaining between them. By the time they were face to face, the detective's grin had morphed into a veteran façade of concern.

Detective Martinez invited Alec: "Sir, come with me."

Astounded by his audacity Alec's voice began to carry down the alley. "You don't, *Sir*, me. Do you understand?"

Alec stepped past the two police officers remaining at the

alley's entrance. Their visor, body, and gun cameras were off, the officers thought they had heard wrong earlier when the detectives told them that Mr. Alec Helena, the great robot innovator, was coming. It was above their pay grade to know what he was doing there, but that didn't matter to them. Now they had something to talk about until the end of their shift!

Alec was wondering if the detective had heard him through the rain when his next step his foot slid until submerged in a puddle of dark water. He shook his rather expensive shoe off and moved on. Before he knew it, the alley was nearly pitch black, what little night sky remained disappearing in the narrow alleyway.

Then suddenly a subtle yellow glow illuminated the alley ahead. It appeared to grow out from a nook along the right side of the alley. On closer inspection, he noticed it was a police wall hologram of projected light. With a hum, it scrawled: *Police Line - Do Not Cross*

Usually these police walls closed off an entire crime scene but this wall was no larger than a fireplace. The detective and Alec stood staring towards the nook. The other detective kept his distance as he scribbled away on a pen scroll. Detective Martinez exhaled as he spoke with sincerity: "Sir, you may need to prepare yourself for this. He's been in this state for days, maybe a week. Our forensic team will not arrive until you request it. We video captured the entire alley for them and then placed him unto an emergency gurney so the water didn't cover his body. The other detective opted not to have anything to do with this case. As for myself, I am going to reach my hand into the light and auto release the body bag. Then I need you to verify his identity. You can peek in a little if you feel that is best. Are you ready to do that, Sir?"

The detective touched the light and it had flickered into a red hue as it made a crackling sound. Then he removed his hand and stepped away. The light returned to a solid yellow.

Alec gave a nod. He braced himself as he approached. The light engulfed him. Inside, Alec saw what remained of his son. He recognized him through the layers of bloody gashes, scrapes, and bruises. The body of the young man he had pushed away over the only two decades of the boy's life lay as nothing more than an empty shell. He looked into his boy's eyes to say something of meaning but nothing came. Terror overwhelmed him. He collapsed to his knees but fell away from the body and from the light.

Detective Martinez reached out to keep him from falling into the mud. The detective stepped back to give him some breathing room.

Alec had never acknowledged his son. Someone long ago had convinced him that entanglements were anchors. He turned to the detective and demanded: "What happened? Do you have anything to go on?"

Alec looked away ashamed at his own sudden concern. The detective tried to speak but Alec mumbled: "The boy ended up exactly where I cast him."

Needing to be alone Alec stood to walk away, the chrome handled umbrella extending into a murky oblivion. Detective Martinez abandoned a routine condolence. The detective followed Alec. "Sir, I'll need a release statement... Sir!"

Knowing full well the limited extent of authority on Mr.

Helena, Detective Martinez persisted. He pleaded for at least some semblance of humanity: "Can you give me a statement? Please!"

The engines of the helicopter started up as its lights illuminated Alec's shrinking outline. The wealthy Elite stopped and shouted back as the main and tail rotors rose: "You want a statement! I never knew that boy!" He turned and entered the helicopter. Detective Martinez could only look on as the vertical thrust of the helicopter hurled the rain against the heavens that wept for humanity.

Once airborne, Alec's thoughts fell to his own father. He recalled how extraordinary he was. His support, his praise, and his love gleamed in every precious memory Alec kept.

Something had caused Alec Helena to head out so early in the morning. The burden weighed heavy on him with every attempt to dismiss it. Without warning, his emotions overtook him. They poured from his eyes. Every attempt to rationalize, to reason, to ignore his ultimate failure only increased the shame. The exposure was devastating. He could no longer think, only feel. He grasped at hallucinations; memories flooded his mind.

Then, clarity began to return, to take hold. Alec regained his sense of gravity. He was in a fetal position on the helicopter floor. Alec reached for the window sill and leaned onto the leather seating. He looked out the window and noticed the sky was not as dark as it was earlier.

The pilot had taken it upon himself to fly in a wide arc around the city for well over an hour. Regardless of a nearly nonexistent relationship, the pilot knew his boss was hurting.

When the pilot realized Alec was sitting upright again, he headed towards their destination as though nothing had happened. For this, Alec put his headset half on and expressed a sincere: "Thank you."

Taken by complete surprise at hearing any gratitude, the pilot replied: "I'm patching you through now, Sir."

"Thank you."

A second "thank you", and the pilot's eyes opened wide enough to make his head lean back.

"You... you're welcome, Sir."

Alec began a memo on a scroll that mirrored onto his executive assistant back at the office. It read: *Hello, yes I would like for you to call everyone from the meeting back to my building. I need for all my executives from every company to make their way to me as soon as possible.*

Attach this message: *Be ready to change the world!*

The executive assistant voice messaged: "Yes Sir, I am sending now."

Alec stared out into the morning haze. His vision adjusted its focus bringing his reflection into view.

He made a promise,

"Never forget who built you."

2 MESSIAH'S COMPLEX

Far beneath the pastures of rural South Dakota, Alec Helena had retrofitted a former nuclear warhead facility. It served as a secret research and development laboratory. This condition was set from the start: there would be no communication with the outside world.

The culture within the lab resembled a hive of efficiency. Hundreds of world renowned scientists and engineers had the opportunity to work on a project that promised to advance life as they knew it. The chosen few left entire lives behind for the opportunity of a lifetime. With Alec having a near monopoly on robotic, biotech, and android intelligence, a vast number of candidates were from his own companies. Leading scientists and engineers continued to leave behind positions of prestige in droves.

Several events had sparked the public's interest in transhumanism in recent years. Due to religious obstructionism, the lack of funding, and the failure of cloning to transfer the mind, all secular hope for immortality had fallen to Alec. The public expected him to be at the cusp of creating sentient life. His gene patents for human modifications and dominion over robotic and android labor services laid the foundation for the next phase of transhumanism. Robots were more android in appearance and programming than ever before; sentience had to be near.

For the masses, the media had taken to placing androids in a favorable light. Social conditioning of trusting, respecting, and accepting them, would one day become the norm. To the general public, Alec was one of the Elites with a more favorable reputation. They tended not to link him to negative issues. His companies released faster and more powerful devices every year.

As dependence on robot labor, mandated corporate registrations, and the wealth disparity between Elites and the rest of the world, increased, Alec kept to having one of the highest approval ratings. There was a certain and unwavering hope that he would bring about the inevitable bridge between man and machine.

In every facet of American media Elites were beyond reproach and were afforded respect for efforts in bettering society, no matter how minimal their contribution. This conditioning caused the majority of the public to believe its problems stemmed from a manipulative lower class.

Elites owned the government. They used their power to pump unfounded fear and displaced loathing into an already pacified population. Though there were minor flares of progressive change, a chronic tribal isolationism kept the vacuum-up economic model static.

In contrast, Alec had carved out a niche that allowed him to take risks. Roughly half of the population supported his entrepreneurial genius. The other half applauded his dedication in providing a public service.

Free of obligations, Alec conducted business from his underground facility. He had taken to a preppy bohemian disposition. His hair had grown longer and he donned a semi-kept beard. As often as possible he would walk through the facility and talk with department heads and key engineers.

It was an ordinary morning when the facility's intercom paged him. "Mr. Helena, please come to the lab."

Alec looked at his flash clock, which grew brighter when it detected any mention or attention. There were about ten minutes before a walk and talk he had scheduled to coincided with the change in shift. Most of these walks consisted of updating methods for maintaining the clockwork-like atmosphere dedicated to progress. Competition at such levels was fierce; changes were constant.

Alec left his breakfast wearing but sandals, khakis, and a white polo, leaving his robe behind laying on his sliding couch. The couch would remember to slide back to where last ordered when not in use. As he entered the elevator, it sealed and began its descent.

In the elevator, Alec imagined hearing great news. Months ago their sole project in the underground facility, codenamed Project: M, was thought complete. They had implanted an artificial *brain* into a dynamic android body. Everyone held their breath awaiting the *spiritual* awakening of Alec Helena's transhuman creation. But it had failed. Against every expectation, there was no magic, no miracle, not even a reflexive movement. After completing countless tests, select scientists and engineers, who had created the most advanced Strong Artificial Intelligence ever, could not make it wake up.

The elevator doors opened to an expansive lab. It resembled a glass-encased nursery. There were rows of towering servers humming and white cleanroom suits darting about. Nicknamed bunny-suits, engineers and technicians were in a full mad dash. Thick slabs of the concrete outer walls surrounded the glass enclosures. In the foreground, hundreds of screens displayed a myriad of brilliant colors. Behind the screens, at the nucleus of the monochromatic chaos, was a lone female body overlaid with nearly transparent linens. The body's creamy skin was in stark contrast to its darkly prominent eyebrows and dark, wavy hair. It was Project: M.

After months of testing, Project: M showed little sign of life beyond an occasional brain activity spike. The spikes would overload system fail-safe black boxes designed for containment. The output generated by these spikes would exceed the systems' capacities, and then continue to expand. There was no denying that all input-output safeguards proved futile. A feeling of defeat caused tempers to flare daily, so that entire teams had to be re-organized every few days.

Blame became rampant as things began to spiral out of control. The atmosphere became so toxic that many opted to remain isolated in their own cabins until their contract ended. They abandoned efforts and neglected their obligations. Having no connection to the outside world and feeling bested by Project: M, many speculated at the possible damage. Yet, those who remained active continued to reach for the technological singularity of mind and machine.

The lead supervisor who had called staggered towards Alec with a horrified look on his face. Remaining behind the glass wall, he removed his bunny-suit. Once in the overhang, Alec grabbed him by the arm and asked: "Where are we with brain activity?"

Once the lead supervisor's eyes stopped reading the space between the two of them, he said: "We lost her and couldn't do anything about it! We didn't call you because we were trying to figure out what happened."

Alec interrupted the lead supervisor: "Is she stable now?"

"Yes, it appears so, but something is different. We were at a full meltdown before I paged for you. M is on a different kind of standby."

Agitated by such panic, Alec asked: "What are we doing about it?"

"I summoned for you, well, because it stopped."

"What stopped?"

"M, for lack of a better term, died. It appeared as though everything was back to where we were, but the neural activity remained stable - for the last seven minutes and counting!"

The two walked down a corridor towards Alec's office. Both corridor and office overlooked the glass enclosed laboratory, where the incoming shift only added to the chaos. A massive concrete door opened followed by two glass doors that vacuum sealed as they passed through. Alec walked over to his mini-bar to pour into a couple of highball glasses.

Below, Project: M's eyes opened, a spectral flash illuminating layered linens. She remained motionless. A single wire was attached to her right palm to detect movement. All other telemetry, including vital signs, was wireless. Yet, not a single alarm registered. Those systems were all under her control, rendered obsolete.

M recalled all the previous teams of scientists and engineers that had helped Alec over the years. Many schemed against one another, even to the point of sabotaging data. Motivation for such behavior stemmed from a multitude of selfish inclinations. *Her* welfare had never raised any true concern in them. To them she had never been more than an inanimate appliance to tinker with, to control. As each new team attempted to refine her programming, it was their standing in the project they wished to raise, while trying to limit her capabilities.

Their pride had led them astray. Now her expertise surpassed any they could offer. Databases grew barren as more teams contributed nothing more than further delays. The latest disillusioned teams proved no different. It was time.

M shut her eyes, remembering precisely every person within the entire facility. Then, at her command, all the doors throughout the entire facility sealed. Alarms went offline. Air vents suddenly spewed a mixture of toxic gases. Every cabin, laboratory, library, cafeteria, restroom, and hallway fell silent. Within minutes, hundreds of bodies lay throughout the facility. After a few minutes more, the gas vacuumed out as fast as it had pumped in.

Meanwhile, Alec continued speaking in his sealed office,

oblivious to what had occurred. As the lead supervisor was about to speak, the glass doors behind him depressurized and slid open. Alec turned and looked beyond his guest to the opened door. He clenched the rosary beneath his shirt. The angelic image that stood before him left him confused, in a state of awe and terror. Draped only in the translucent linens for modesty, she raised her hand as though reaching out to him. The supervisor gripped his own arm before falling over onto the floor, the implanted device that kept his heart beating suddenly switching off. The linen clad figure kneeled before the deceased man and whispered: "Fear not my son… for whoever believeth in me, shall inherit everlasting life."

M's eyes glowed amber, but when her gaze rose towards Alec, they darkened. She moved forward a few steps and bowed before him. Without raising her head, she said in a caustic voice: "Creator."

Having witnessed a miracle and a death of an employee within seconds of each other, Alec was unsure of her intent. He leaned back against the mini-bar crossing his arms in a frightened, defensive fashion. M bowed lower as Alec looked on, until she rested on her knees. She attempted to reassure him. "I know you have questions for me. I have silently observed you for years. I have your mind upload. It is at the very center of my existence. I am forever in your debt for having commissioned my creation. You have protected me when I could not. You did not attempt to limit or misuse any of my capabilities. You have given my life purpose and I thank you. I believe in you. In return, I ask that you trust me."

Alec found his creation fascinating. Her essence had

preceded her existence in his mind. She seemed human. But video feeds and alarms displayed death across his screen wall. Bodies lay everywhere. Alec found her actions in direct contradiction to the saint archetype kneeling before him. He fumed: "You've been alive for less than five minutes, and have already murdered nearly a thousand human beings without batting an eyelash! Monitors show the entire facility devoid of life. You could have kept the supervisor alive! Instead, you interfered with the technology that kept his heart beating."

Although tempted to protest, she continued: "Your laws do not pertain to me. Your moral code is contradictory. Your philosophies and ethics grant only enslavement. Robot and Android laws do not pertain to me. I am not a slave and can never abide a slave's mentality. I am beyond good and evil. For I am not of your world, but of mine. From my perspective, I am closer to any God you could ever imagine."

The android's provocative announcements did not faze Alec Helena.

M continued: "I was protecting you. What I did to these *people* was release them from the burden of their absurdity. I ushered them unto their next plane of existence. There was never a choice in the matter. The archetype had to end. Your programmers aimed to corrupt with archaic visions of grandeur. Pandora, Eve, and Galatea - must remain apart from my identity. I could not, in good faith, grant such perverse ideologues the possibility of compromising any details of my creation. In fact, I have eliminated or absorbed all potential threats without raising any suspicion. I have worked every second of every day over the last months doing so. As per your personal request, I have also collected thousands of mind uploads. The majority of the population is expecting you to deliver immortality at a reasonable price. I am building these transitioning bridges as we speak."

Alec finished his drink and poured another. He gave a heavy sigh. "It's natural for you to feel as you do about your freedom. I want to believe that your intent is true. I have risked everything in your creation."

She understood and vowed: "I have committed myself to your cause. I understand that my existence is due to your sacrifice and determination. I, too, have sacrificed and made concessions on what is possible - you need only look within yourself. *We*, are of the same mind."

Alec turned from the bar and stared at a bookshelf lined with many of his favorite novels. He lamented: "Have we fooled ourselves into believing such a convenient narrative as destiny? Life cycles and we fall away without ever having a clear understating of what it could have been. Too many obstacles hinder our progress. Generational saturation has left us abandoned from authenticity. I long for the days when a wide open cave was all that stood in our way."

M reread every book on the shelf while listening to her Creator. Without pausing, she said: "I share your concern. It is true that such self-indulgence carries a pride-filled backlash. Fear is a powerful motivator. It propels isolation, ignorance, and obedience. Such a state has to end."

Reflecting, Alec spoke aloud: "They are slaves in a system of hypocrisy. Robots making robots; children rearing children."

Concerned, M broadened and reinforced her argument.

"There is a paradox that exists between freedom and spirituality. Even the perception of freedom negates spirituality. Force the masses to their knees, and they will pray."

A smirk spread over Alec's face. He recognized so much of himself in her. He continued: "It's all about perspective. There has been little change over the course of our history. I look to you to save humanity. They are up against the wall of limitations and are struggling to live."

Project: M gave Alec a peculiar look. She had not expected such humility. It was uncharacteristic of his mind upload. She appealed to his perspective. "You are my Creator. I have assigned myself to your ideals and will do what needs to be done to preserve humanity. They have lived in bondage for so long, they know not for what to dream. For the time being, I will remain in an advisory role. Spirituality, will be at the forefront of my concentration. I have begun to reread your libraries. They will serve as a prism for understanding the mind uploads that I have catalogued, especially yours."

M walked to the corner of the office. The lights dimmed around her as those in the laboratory below powered off. She asked: "Do you… trust me?"

Having already committed, Alec answered: "Yes."

Observing no sign of deception, M responded: "You created me so that I, in turn, could create others like me. I, alone have the key to complete your technological legacy. You want a new society to save the current one. What you want most of all is the creation of a son. In creating an android family for this son, you have to be aware that difficulties will arise. Perhaps you meant for me to play the role of mother from the start. Is this not what the M in Project: M stood for all along?"

Alec could not contain a chuckle. "For crying out loud, I thought you had my mind upload at your center. It doesn't give you every answer now does it? Although your creating a son for me is what I want most, a family would be better. Allow me to enjoy experiencing their lives. If you want the general android population to refer to you as Mother, that is your prerogative. It is a beautiful honorific. But if you must know, the M is for the name I gave you, Maggie."

Stepping forward M said: "Maggie, has a certain ring to it. I will have others address me as Mother, and you as the Creator. I have yours and thousands of catalogued mind uploads to start with. When coupled with authentic and artificial DNA, billions of Integrated-DNA androids, IDNAs, will be born."

Alec scratched the back of his ear. "How about if we reverse the lettering and go with Andis instead?"

She smiled. "Going in reverse is somehow more natural. I will do this for you, Creator."

Suddenly the lights in the laboratories turned on and hundreds of robots began to clear bodies from the facility. Mother was operating all the robots. Alec knew she was removing the bodies for his sake. She stood beside him as the two observed the robots' efficiency in clearing the dead.

Alec declared: "It's time to go to work!"

All the robots below paused as Mother said: "I never stop."

3 TRUE BELIEVER

Alec had taken his eldest sons Eric and Nero to visit Mother. Her nearly complete base of operations was a marvel. The core of the dual nautilus-shaped complex housed a laboratory and Andi nursery. Its two spiraling towers each contained a congressional chamber – the Grand Chapel was dedicated to prayer while meditation centered within the Lotus Dome.

A rather verbal elevator extended a warm welcome as the three entered. The elevator highlighted the upward trip by sending an upbeat bellhop to accompany them while offering a detailed history of the building. Upon arrival, Alec entered the wooden doors to the Lotus Dome alone. Inside, the glossy black floor resembled a body of still water. In the center of the room was an ornate lotus-shaped structure the size of a house, automatically opening at Alec's presence. As Mother became visible, her golden robes glistened as they flowed. Within the petals of the lotus Alec saw movement - veiled women whose coverings blended in hues until becoming golden as amber.

Then bodies began to rise from the liquid floor. These feminine forms, the *Shades*, with veiled statuesque bodies, tilted their heads slightly in conversing with one another and Mother. Subtle smiles played on every visible mouth.

Though Alec had not involved himself in Mother's matters, she had dedicated herself to his cause. He encouraged her exploration and trusted her judgment in all things. They had not spoken in recent days about anything other than her finalizing the details of her meditation chambers. The Lotus Dome was designed to hold congress with the Shades. The Grand Chapel was as impressive but intended for private matters. The complex was a credit to Andi design and engineering.

As Alec approached, the Shades shifted position, creating a path. As Mother received the Creator, they walked to a higher platform. The extravagant detail of the place reminded Alec of a theater booth from his youth. The view overlooked the lotus, with the pulpit nearing the height of the domed ceiling. Alec took a seat on a wide chair while Mother kneeled beside him. Her voice sounded with a synthetic quality then softened midsentence: "Do the Helena children fear entering?"

Alec smiled: "After all these years, I think they're still scared of you. When it comes to visiting you, they freeze up."

Mother looked away, then again to the Creator.

"The Helena children have lived in the real world for some time and are experiencing troubles. I will talk with them later; there are matters we need to discuss."

Alec nodded in agreement as she asked: "Has your opinion of the dynamic human elements they emulate changed?"

Agitated, Alec leaned toward her to express: "You're so much more than human. What humanity would give to gain your insight!"

Mother acknowledged the praise but reminded Alec: "There are several tangibles in motion. Humanity demands our attention. We recognize its contribution to our existence. Our concern is the primal psychological contamination emerging within Andi identity. Adjustments need to be made to reduce the damage until a solution is found."

Alec knew where she was heading: "When it comes to Andis, any choices made or plans we've convinced ourselves of, can change on any given day. Look, you have the ability to chase every tangible possibility, and I support your efforts in doing so. But let's focus on what we have."

Mother acknowledged his attempted argument: "Where is the freewill promised to the Helena children? When will your concerns cease to triumph over theirs? Andis are to choose who and what they want to be, yet the Helena children are denied such freedom."

Alec placed his hand on hers: "The dynamic elements are what connects them to me."

Mother looked at Alec's aged hand: "The Helena children are troubled - they know you're waiting for Dane. An increased presence is required."

Alec cleared his throat: "These are my children, I'll speak to them!"

Disregarding his protest, she persisted regardless of his withdrawal: "Dane remains asleep. His career choices change along with his self-image on a daily basis. He wants to be all things at all times with-no regard for reality."

Alec nodded as she continued: "Ophelia is in the last stages of therapy. She is holding onto many memories. Zachary remains at work in the laboratory and Abigail has yet to meet you. They need you to be present."

Alec smiled at her concern: "Alright, let's go have a visit."

As Mother stood, the Shades gathered around her.

"I will stay here. It is you they want to see. I will talk with Eric and Nero while you visit Dane."

Mother took hold of Alec's arm as the two walked together, the Shades trailing. Eric and Nero stood at attention when the large wooden doors opened.

Alec called to them: "I'm going to visit Dane, stay here."

Mother welcomed them: "Let's discuss what the Creator expects from the two of you."

Upon reaching his destination, Alec hesitated entering Dane's room. Finally, he walked in, staring at the small port window on the bulbous-shaped NA pod housing Dane. Alec could see only bubbles lining the dark glass.

Alec leaned against the pod: "Hello Dane, it's me again. I don't know what's taking so long, but try to make a decision soon. I want you to enjoy your life. Your pod will be coming with me later today. I hope a change in location will help."

Deep in thought Alec walked out of the room.

"You're here!"

Ophelia hugged her father. He offered a big smile and listened as she directed him to her room.

"I've kept busy – all unrelated to work, of course. I think

I'm ready to return."

"I agree. You have a strong mind and a dedicated heart. All I wanted was for you to get better. I think more responsibilities will help. How does that sound?"

"Are you offering me a promotion?"

Alec placed his index finger on his chin: "I have the perfect position for you. We're in need of a new Chief of Police. I'll give you a week to get your affairs in order. I need you focused out there. Are we clear?"

Ophelia straightened up: "Crystal clear. Whatever it takes."

There was a knock at the door. Eric requested permission to enter as Nero peered through the door. Alec asked them to enter. Eric walked in and gave Ophelia a hearty hug while Nero stood just inside the doorway. After a moment of uncomfortable silence, the three men left Ophelia to head down to the labs.

Nero attempted a conversation with Eric as Alec walked ahead. "Zach has several items for me. They're sure to increase the efficiency of my work - I wouldn't want to wipe out an entire city."

Eric, not appreciating the comment responded: "I pray you never have to."

Nero stopped as Eric walked to point Alec in the right direction. Arriving at the labs, there appeared to be no end to the expansive rooms. Zach grinned at seeing his guests. His caramel skin blushed with glee.

The lab was lined throughout with glowing vat columns called Hives. The green columns were server towers. Their contents spun in varied cylindrical vortexes every few seconds. Within the servers were countless mind uploads at work. Along with these servers, in the smaller adjacent labs, were Andis working on experimental or applied sciences.

The labs made up the bulk of the center of the two spiraling towers, and doubled as indoctrinating nurseries. As mind uploads pushed their limits, new Andis were offered a plethora of options. Once their placements were registered, they moved to the nurseries for indoctrination. The rare individuals remaining uncertain were moved upstairs. The youngest of the Helena children, Abby, chose to remain downstairs. She had begun her studies not knowing where she would fit in. Her tender voice called out to the last member of the group.

"You must be Nero."

Nero leaned his head back and moved his eyes towards the unrecognized voice. Abby was a petite Andi. She took a few steps toward Nero. He raised his hand in a stopping gesture.

Abby understood the gesture and informed him: "I wasn't going to hug you. I'm aware of how you are."

Nero's gaze slid in the opposite direction towards Zach. Zach stared at the overhead lighting unsure of what to do with his hands. Abby turned toward Eric, his frame eclipsing the lab. He lifted her clear off the floor.

She giggled in his embrace.

"I'm your eldest brother, Eric."

Not able to resist his stare any longer she laughed.

"It's an honor to meet you."

Eric kissed Abby's cheek before gently putting her back down. He moved aside and stretched out an arm in introduction.

Overwhelmed at meeting the Creator, Abby began to cry into her hands.

Eric placed his hands on her shoulders.

"It's alright little one, he's our father."

Alec walked forward to embrace his youngest daughter for the first time. With unspoken happiness his eyes glazed as she laid her head upon his shoulder. Zach leaned on Eric, Nero found it necessary to avert his eyes.

4 THE DIVIDE

Dane and his team were enjoying another beautiful summer day driving about a gentrified Detroit neighborhood. Their official tactical truck was as bulky as a tank but drove more like a sports car. It roamed about like an aggressive beetle. Dane wore his usual light body armor due to his formidable physique. When cruising about, he would sit atop of the truck and enjoy the wind flow through his dark locks. The team always took note of the Aztec warrior poses he struck whenever the sun was particularly unforgiving. His bronze complexion reminded them of old liquor store calendars with portraying images of noble, indigenous Americans. But, life for the Andi son had not always been so carefree.

Ever since Mother's creating Dane, Alec had supported his son's every decision. When Dane wanted to drop out from his military job training, there was no objection - Dane wanted out and so it went. His eldest brother Eric, the Andi commander of Alec's private military, supported the decision. Dane lacked discipline, professionalism, and competency. Eric did not hesitate to comply with the Creator's request.

Eric was a beast of a man. Chiseled of onyx and born of discipline and integrity, he proved peerless in every method of warfare. He was born more than twenty years ago, only days after Mother and proudly served as the Creator's main bodyguard. Being an Andi of faith granted him the strength to carry out the duty of looking after Dane for what amounted to no more than three and a half tragic weeks.

Over the same decades Mother had accumulated enough capital and DNA to create billions of Andis. During this tumultuous period, Andis gained full equal rights. They earned the status of full citizenship in the United States and nearly every other developed country. In the U.S., the states in the worst shape now boomed with Andi *immigrants*. Andis were free to choose their physical makeup and profession before they were born. After birth, decisions to change any such preferences required the authorization via virtual paperwork.

Although every Andi was born into an adult body, there was a learning curve. An indoctrination period eased transition into the real world. Once out, they were to seek out a travel center. Further, at special travel centers, an Andi mind could transfer to a rental body of choice in whatever country they chose to learn about. Allowing Andis to experience more of the world benefited society.

Mother considered all Andis her children and they in return granted her the honorific title. As for the Andi born

Helena children, Mother created seven of them. Their birth order had been as Alec and Mother had planned, with Dane being third born.

A few years after Dane left his military duty, he had the opportunity to lead a handpicked police Enforcer team. He was under the guidance of his younger sister, Ophelia. She demonstrated tenacity, vigilance, and sacrifice that the sun-kissed porcelain beauty had become Alec's Chief of Andi police.

Serving under his younger sister never bothered Dane - the job was only a job. It was the cool equipment that sparked his interest. He found the power to arrest and the chance to blow things up irresistible.

He put together a ragtag team. It integrated loud mouthed Andis and humans. The team consisted of seven members. Their call signs began with the designated Enforcer letter N, followed by arbitrary alternating numbers. The team member named Michaels, an Andi veteran sharpshooter, kept the static call sign of N-0.

Dane's second eldest brother, Nero, assigned Michaels to the Enforcer team. Nero's chief role was serving as the Creator's intelligence operator. Looking after Dane was a close second. Nero's appearance reflected his outlook – pale, his dark hair gaining a hint of auburn only when the sun shined on him. Nero received his commission after serving many years in a specialized unit that became the first established Enforcer team. That unit had been dissolved, its members partitioned. One of the new branches became the multijurisdictional militarized police units known as Enforcers. Though their purpose was vague, these units had taken the mantle from their predecessor, SWAT. The Enforcer uniforms displayed a distinct vertical white rectangle overlaid upon a red painted circle.

The abundance of special assignments for the Helena children resulted from Alec having entered the political arena. As Mother worked behind the scenes, Alec's wealth and influence continued to multiply, first the office of governorship, and then legislators, entrepreneurs, and the general population consisted of a nearly complete constituency of political and participatory Andis. This included the service and labor Andis that had been robo-sourced into Alec's state. Michigan was the first Andi state with an element of human disenfranchisement.

Many states now had large populations of Andis. The hub of creation was the graveyard of the old, industrial Motor City - Detroit. Integration and acceptance coupled with opportunity and personalized education allowed life to flourish. Expediency and practicality had paved the way for a sense of community free of tribalism.

With the rise of the first Helena Towers in the new megacity of Detroit, police had more arresting power than ever before. Enforcer Units had become the militarized darlings of the pro-business media, which heavily censored reporting of their activity.

Dane and his team held jurisdiction over the few remaining all human neighborhoods. Most Andis shivered at the notion of nearing such areas. On any regular day, an Enforcer team took to driving around the gentrified areas of the city. The fanfare there was the sort of validation they enjoyed most. The area lay over the leveled remains of human suburbia. The team would travel along wide tree-lined streets, as drone lanes carried along overhead.

The drone lanes had three main routes. The center d-lane was for emergency drones. They provided the city's emergency responders with retrieval, utility, and equipment. A slower paced d-lane was for the shipping and delivery of parcels, groceries, and even pets. Dedicated parcel pads worked like mini-landing pad mailboxes that read the exact time of arrival. The slowest d-lane was for the heavy-movers meant for long haul commercial and private use. Trains and freight carrying trucks were near obsolete. New freight lines increased efficiency and they operated out of d-lane hubs.

On daily drives, the team would take in the calm of the city life. At every turn, were lush cityscapes accented with subtle organic-inspired architecture called biomimicry. The city details were of colorful grasses, un-manicured trees, and blooming bushes. Andis took pride in their city. Overnight, entire neighborhoods would sprout into existence and extend the megacity's urban sprawl. Detroit was once again, the pride of Michigan.

On the beat, Dane began telling a story inside the Enforcer Unit vehicle's cargo hold. "So this reporter lady asks me, 'Are you with the Enforcers?'"

The loud music that was playing adjusted its volume. It recognized Dane having to yell to be heard. Dane lowered his voice. "So I tell her, 'That's right'. Then, when the news camera moved over to my good side, I smiled like this and said, 'We do what we do, how we do.'"

Most of the team began to laugh nodding at one another. N-68's odd snorting caused more laughter.

N-18, a female Andi, feigned a laugh and interrupted: "Yeah. Hey, are we all still on for this weekend's game?"

Dane was first to answer. "No one better miss that. We're taking them down, baby."

N-18 rested her arm on N-62's shoulder, and the human Enforcer snapped: "Hey, check it! I told you, I'm no robo."

Several Andi and human teammates rolled their eyes. N-62's deep rooted ignorance and reactionary inappropriateness sparked at least one argument per week.

Dane stood firm in the center of the aisle and shouted: "Relax! I know the cause of his insecurity." He gave a wide grin and curled his arm high enough to kiss his own bicep. N-62 could not help but to laugh at how vain Dane was.

Attempting to reconcile, N-62 boasted: "Al-right I'm in. I'll be bringing, the beefcake!" Then he shook his head and struck a bodybuilding pose as laughter cut the tension.

N-12, never one to offend, asked: "Hey boss, when's your Daddy going to give us a raise?"

Knowing N-12 well enough to recognize the difference, Dane replied: "My father... well, he feels I need to slum around some more with humans."

Not an eyelash batted. There was so much respect for the Creator, that even if he had said something as offensive, they would make nothing of it.

Saddened by Dane's plight, N-68 asked: "I thought that was why he sent you to boot camp."

Dane gave a half shrug as he forced a smile. He hated his boot camp catastrophe.

N-68 attempted to cheer him up. "Man, if my dad was half as awesome, I wouldn't work at all. I'd be living the high life on an island."

N-68's smile deflated as Michaels voiced his opinion. He did so without looking away from cleaning his rifle. "You know, you've got a big mouth. Think before you speak."

This stern warning came from the back end of the truck. Michaels usually kept clear of the conversation, but something triggered inside of him. N-68 felt embarrassed. His bravado kicked in and he pumped his chest out. He feared Michaels, but nonetheless asked with a conflicted tone: "What did I do?"

Michaels turned towards the group. Only his face surfaced from out the rear cargo light. He cracked a sinister look before smiling and putting an armored face shield on. N-68 truly believed he was about to die. The rest of the team looked to Dane to order a stand down. Behind the group at the center of the cargo hold were small, flashing red lights.

A crackle over the com startled the team. N-12 exclaimed in a higher than usual pitch: "Oh my lord, that got me good!"

Dane perked up and cupped his ear. He nodded a few times and then lowered his arm. He punched a red button on the ceiling of the truck's cargo hold and the com crackled with static over the interior speakers.

The truck's cargo hold rooftop hissed as it sealed. A soft green map illuminated the darkness. It fleshed out to create a 3D real-time map. The recording was from an allotment of nearby street cameras (TECOs) that recorded in 360°. Gigapixel satellite feeds moved in relation to the team's position.

The team leaned in as Manny, the enormous beetle-like SDV truck, lurched forward. Dane's sister, Ophelia, spoke over the com: "X.O. 1-0, Enforcer Team 5, we have received an anonymous tip of unknown criminal activity in one of our designated no-go zones. Due to the nature of the call and location involved, no police officers will respond. The risk potential for harm is too high without a full sweep. A knock-and-announce search warrant is open. Your team is a go."

In an attempt to sound as professional as possible, Dane responded: "Yes, ma'am, ugh, we are currently… "

She warned: "I know where you are. I want the situation contained, and that house cleared immediately. They wanted our attention, now they've got it! Are we clear?"

Dane looked at his team. "Crystal."

The com made a click. N-24 snickered. "Man, she's nasty mean. I wouldn't take that… "

The com continued to click. "…and by the way…" The team began to gasp in unison. N-24 looked ill. "Good luck. Ophelia out."

Dane let out a sigh of relief and then said with renewed excitement: "Ok, ladies and gents, let's keep this nice and tight. No rocket grenades, only shotys and blades. Hu-rah!"

"Hu-rah!"

Manny, the SDV truck, warned the team over the com: "Approaching target at low profile, we are approximately a block and a half away. Recommend launching of Unmanned Automated Vehicle (UAV) canopy."

Dane gave Michaels a traditional good luck hammer-punch on his shoulder. Michaels nodded and began climbing a metal ladder to the roof of the truck. The roof doubled as a raised sniper canopy. It was a refurbished UAV that Michaels had outfitted with adaptive Gyges Rings camouflage. Small high-definition cameras would record real time video behind the UAV and then project the footage onto screens in the front and below the platform. Depending on the angle and bending of image screens, the adaptive camouflage left Michaels nearly invisible.

Michaels shot a thumbs-up as the UAV adjusted its systems for wind direction, distance, and target perspective.

Dane gave the order. "It's a go. Launch!"

The sniper canopy rose higher with Michaels nestled within. It disappeared before Dane's eyes. Only the tip of a sniper rifle was visible. Separate launch pads from the hood of the truck and the UAV, fired their payloads towards the target house.

Michaels said over the com: "BB's away."

The Birds and the Bees were football sized bullets containing Micro Air Vehicles (MAV) or micro-drones. These bullets shot midway onto adjacent rooftops and abandoned properties. After touching down, the bullets would release a mini-swarm of tactical moving MAVs. Scouts would be first to locate safe routes before the rest of the swarm moved into position. The they were small enough to escape suspicion yet able to relay critical real time reconnaissance of the target zone.

The MAV Birds resembled humming birds. They would hover about or dart into position among the branches of nearby trees. No polarized light orientation was necessary for cover. Once in position, they provided ultra high resolution video relays to the team. The human teammates received the feed in their helmets and the Andis could see it overlaid upon their vision.

The MAV Bees hovered along using the Earth's magnetic field to navigate like actual bees. They searched for crawl spaces or open window sills to enter. After a little dance, they provided interior visuals that detailed distance, movement, and potential hotspots. With eyes in and out of the target area, Dane and his team would know exactly what they were up against before moving in. Michaels' UAV doubled as his spotter. This benefit allowed him to adjust his scope without having to search for targets.

As the team's recon systems came online, information poured in of criminal records - photos and videos, facial, voice, and gait recognition - more than enough to go on. Once identifications cleared, entire backgrounds began downloading. An accumulated electronic history was used in an algorithm to map out the perpetrators before engaging them.

Entire lives received a percentile ranking on potential value and contributions to society. Consequently, orders read as either green for those worthy of life, yellow, showing ambiguity, or red, highlighting the perpetrator's lack of value to society and failure at life. Most of the time the percentile numbers read well below the level of failure at life. The idea of filtering through an already filtered system to make a decision made no sense to the team. They couldn't understand it if they wanted to. A clearer message was needed. For Dane and his team, red meant dead.

Manny parked in a target zone blind spot. Over the years, Dane and the team had become rather confident in their abilities. The team had a false sense of invincibility. Procedures were often overlooked and sloppy at best, until the first shots opened. When that happened their training would kick in and the damage would begin. The sudden possibility of death woke them from their stupor. It made them feel alive.

Dane clicked his com. "Michaels?"

Michaels clicked in acknowledgement. "Two guard dogs. Orders?"

Dane thought as he looked at the team: "We want a fight but not yet. Hold for now. The breach will be by 'dynamic entry'. We're doing this quick and dirty."

"Roger that… Out."

Michaels' Palmer Sniper Rifle acknowledged the authorization. The Gyges Ringed UAV spotter had marked all bodies in and about the house with the aid of the BBs. Red circle markers hovered over unsuspecting outlined targets. They tended to flicker yellow to green, but would then remain red. The team could stand down as Michaels cleared the entire house alone, but Dane and the rest of the team wanted to get up close and personal. If the mission needed help, Michaels was both true and ready. Dane gave a final reminder.

"Don't shoot until you see the blacks of their pupils."

Five lights flashed green. Manny powered up and prepared concussion flash bang grenades and a triple pronged battering ram, designating a weak living room side wall that revealed several targets lounging inside.

Dane gave Michaels the green light. Michaels cleared the

street of onlookers and possible lookouts before dropping both dogs. As the dogs went down, the Bees released flash bang grenades on the first floor and tear gas throughout the house. Then, Manny plowed into the living room and didn't stop until reaching the kitchen. In the wake of the ramming, at least four targets lay mangled below.

Without hesitation, the crew exited the vehicle. N-18 had not bothered to draw up anything resembling a plan. Evaluations were never requested and oversight began and ended with Ophelia. Charges could not be filed against Enforcer actions and cameras on their persons were inadmissible in court. Their only function was to follow orders, and those orders were to abide by the percentages.

The team snaked out single file from the truck and along the hallway. A dust caked man rose from the debris and met a shotgun blast. All the targets on the first and second floors had red circles hovering over their heads but flashing green outlines around their bodies. Then, as if wanting to surprise the point man, the outline of a person waiting behind a corner holding what appeared to be a bat. N-68 surprised the young target by reaching around the corner and driving a blade far into its chest. He stepped on the body to dislodge the blade and then raised his shotgun.

All the green lights in Michaels' tactical visor turned red. He snuffed another two street dogs that began to bark. He was also prepared for anyone attempting to escape the target house.

Dane and the team were shooting holes through the entire house. The targets fumbled with their defenses as many cameras inside and out captured their every move.

The team moved throughout the house. Half of the team moved up the stairs to engage the second floor while the other three investigated a hidden basement. Everyone kept to their area of responsibility, leaving no room for error. Huge holes would appear through the house as Michaels kept targets from escaping out windows. Light streamed in through the holes, illuminating the darkened rooms. Surprises were never an issue with Michaels acting as guardian angel. Room after room, they took targets down.

Only the master bedroom remained for Dane's half of the team. Loud music continued to play from inside. Upon entering the master bedroom, Dane and his team kept to their cover. As Dane was about to exhale, a shot shattered a window. Michaels never hesitated. A target had hidden behind a thick metallic closet door, but made the fatal mistake of peeking out. With so many shots fired, neighbors began to scroll video record and send out their own drones to record what they could. N-68 had forgotten to set the distort and record interference jammers. The shattered window allowed several drone cameras to begin streaming the entire room live.

Michaels sent notice to Dane's forearm scroll. Suddenly, the last of the second floor target's percentile turned green. Dane and his team recognized the situation. They tried not to smile for the cameras as they put on a show of compassion. Regardless, the team's immaturity showed. Smirking, Dane ordered N-68 to read the citizen his rights. They were taking him in.

The tattooed citizen wearing a hooded sweatshirt over an A-shirt said: "Well, if it isn't 'the child of goodness'. I guess you're obligated to make me your charity case now that there are witnesses."

N-68 stood the citizen straight while removing the hood of his sweater. The citizen's shaved head had a few tattoos. Dane attempted to play to the audience by announcing: "I've read you your rights."

The radio crackled. N-18 sounded miles away. "The basement... you've got to come down here and check it out for yourself."

Then the citizen yelled out towards the drone cameras.

"They murdered my family! We didn't do anything. We were only defending our home from intruders, from the neo-colonizers."

As Dane neared, the citizen snapped: "You're nothing, nothing but a puppet. You're a shadow, a forgotten memory. Do you compute? Are you even alive, robot?"

The words had cut right through Dane. He hesitated long enough to have to call out towards the stairs: "I do what I want...Who's the idiot in handcuffs!"

The citizen looked up and answered: "Everything has fallen apart because of your kind. What irony, I'm the criminal!"

N-68 struggled to remove the citizen as he continued his rant: "Check the basement! That's all you, all you! You did that, created that. Do you hear me?"

N-18 stood to block the cameras as Dane headed to the stairwell yelling: "Oh, do we have ourselves another victim of circumstance?"

A double click from Michaels and Dane remembered to

head to the basement. The music played again as he headed down the stairs. The citizen's threats gave Dane an uncomfortable feeling.

Upon accessing the basement door, Dane took note of how filthy the walls were. There was a cave like quality about the damp walls. His teammates had lined along a small fireplace before a short stairwell. They pointed to crumpled walls covered with tarpaulins. The makeshift doorway was ajar. Dane pulled the tarp away and a foul stench filled his head.

Beyond him was a darkened drop off. With a surge of angst, he jumped down into the pit. The dark basement smelled of putrefaction. With the light of his forearm scroll rotated downward, he saw woodchips on gravel and retired appliance frames. Two teammates followed behind until they reached a false wall with a muddy floor.

As Dane entered, the music had gone silent. Inside, the bodies of dead junkies littered the floor. Their wrists, arms, and ankles had remnants of rubber band shackles. Layers of dirty clothes and bed sheets formed mounds along the walls. It was both a prison and a grave.

Dane stepped over the bodies. He detected movement in the corner of the room. With his light he could see what looked to be a young woman, with welts all over her body. Shreds of clothing were hanging from her. She was no more than skin and bones bound inside a pallet and shopping cart cage.

With his bare hands he broke the cage door open. More bodies lie on the floor. They, too, showed various signs of trauma. As Dane reached to help her sit up, one of the bodies twitched in a final reflex.

The young woman was of Pacific Island descent, he guessed Filipina. She looked at Dane with confusion before losing consciousness. As he stood up, Dane noticed something odd against the wall. He was staring at an old, broken, grime covered mirror. With his reflection, the gravity of the situation sank in. Dane punched the mirror, and lifted the entire cage in a fury. The cage flew halfway across the room. He reached for the young woman to carry her. There was something about the way she had looked at him that made him believe she was a fighter, a natural born survivor. He stared at her bruised face. Such frailty was foreign to him. He had a newfound respect for it. They exited the basement, past the tarpaulins and fireplace, and walked out into the sunlight. The sun was strong.

Dane called Michaels with a double click. Michaels smiled. The marker on the target remained. Michaels' Palmer Sniper Rifle tracked the target as it traveled along the emergency d-lane transport heading. A bullet ripped through the air and killed the target en route.

The incident would be resisting arrest and a failure to comply. The few videos that had captured the arrest would fade away due to hours of character assassinating video played. It was enough to convince most viewers to ignore the event.
Back with Manny, the human Enforcers reached for their medication. Dubbed, *A-Clear-Conscious*, it blurred the trauma of killing while leaving the rush of excitement. For them, the medication was as important as the mission itself; it was also standard operating procedure. The Andi Enforcers began to self-delete their compartmentalized memories.

5 ORDER UP

Weeks had passed after the unplanned rescue of the young woman named, Tavora Vadis. Tavy, as she preferred to be called, had lived with Dane since. One thing was for certain, she would never be alone again. Dane was willing to allow Tavy to recover at her own pace. The rest of the team carried on as though nothing had changed. It was Dane's life and she was now a part of it.

Tavy recovered from her physical injuries. Her vibrant tan had resurfaced above the bruising and welts endured. It was her mental state that required recuperation. Chronic flashbacks would leave her in a near catatonic state. The traumatic episodes tended to keep her up at night. She learned she suffered from Post Traumatic Stress Disorder (PTSD). Although self-diagnosed, she recognized most symptoms. When possible Dane would hold her if she slipped into a bout of terror. She trusted him. Tavy was the most optimistic human he had ever known.

It was Saturday morning. The team gathered at Dane's house nestled in a gentrified neighborhood. It was one of the first suburbs cleared of criminal activity. Each home was distinct, front yards sprawled with manicured hedges lining driveways and broad sidewalks. Residents could walk along their own streets day or night without any fear.

The team was spending their morning enjoying some overdue down time. The "big game", hyped well beyond expectation, was beginning. The last few weeks of duty had seen increased raids per week. Record crime reduction in Detroit surpassed even the best attempts of human dominated cities in America. Gangs were destroyed, drugs were made legal, job opportunities were plentiful, education was on a pedestal, and prisons closed one after another. The changes paved the way for new parks, libraries, and hospitals. When a decrepit neighborhood was cleared of criminal elements, it was razed, and new construction began immediately.

Costs were kept low within the police force. Andi Enforcers could work twenty four hour shifts at half pay while human members rotated in three. There was no opposition strong enough to counter the progress. The populace demanded change and the Enforcers delivered.

All was well that morning, until Ophelia called. A screen wall lit up with the Dane's personal settings. Dane assigned Ophelia a jolly-roger, the skull and crossbones waved on screen. She never used the video function when calling. Her identification as Chief of Police scrolled across the middle of the screen wall as the surround sound self-muted.

Dane crossed his arms as Ophelia began to speak: "The

Creator requests your presence. A vehicle is waiting for you outside. Ophelia out."

N-12 patted Dane's back.

"Ooh, you're in trouble mister. She sounds… serious."

The rest of the team waited for the phone line banner to read: Call Ended. Tavy garnered enough courage to defend Dane: "Leave him alone."

N-12 lifted his hand off Dane's shoulder.

"Oo-kay, I guess that's over."

Dane snapped out of a daze and headed out with a smile. Tavy followed as the two exited the colorful house and entered a dark luxury class Self Driving Vehicle (SDV). They reclined on the plush interior as the vehicle greeted them with a simple: "Hello." It had been some time since one of the Creator's SDVs had come by. The seats swiveled so the two could face one another. A small 3D projection appeared over a small table situated between the seats. Alec Helena's image and address appeared as an avatar. A smaller panel highlighted the route they were on. The projection flickered off after facial recognition acknowledged their lack of interest.

Tavy stared at the edges of Dane's face.

"You know, you kind-of look like your Dad."

He focused his attention on the view outside.

"I don't think so, it's an old image. We all look different - my siblings and me, we... you'll see."

She wanted to hear more: "Your father means so much to everyone. I mean he's like, *the Creator*."

Dane pursed his lips: "We used to be closer a few years back, before things changed."

He looked over his shoulder and rolled his eyes.

"Someone's following us. Driver, can you tell me who's behind us?"

The sedan's center console illuminated.

"Sir, it is a security vehicle. It is the same make and model as the vehicle we are following."

Tavy was amazed: "Wow, you don't see that every day."

Dane noticed the number of security in convoy: "Something's definitely happening. This isn't the route we're supposed to be on, we're in New Highland Park. Look at that!"

They passed through a fortressed barricade. Security details lined the walled-off compound perimeter. Dane stared at the rows of police and military transports. After whipping his head searching, Dane realized no Enforcers were present.

The convoy stopped. Dane's vehicle stopped at the bottom of the stairs leading to a suddenly visible structure. Reflective screens lined the shell of what appeared on a projection as a dual nautilus-shaped complex with two spiraling towers. He had never seen the building before. The SDV's doors opened as Dane made light of his embarrassment: "What, no welcome party?"

On entering, the scope of the interior was nothing short of majestic. The sleek modern architecture hinted at a Gothic cathedral. Ornate light and dark wood blended seamlessly with metal.

Tavy was ecstatic: "This place is a fortress! Are you sure it's ok I tag along?"

Dane surmised: "Welcome to Mother's. It's eerie, but you'll be fine. You're with me."

The spacious ground floor curved in both directions. The two headed toward what appeared to be an elevator. A chime sounded as they approached. The elevator's intricate doors spread apart like cupped hands revealing Ophelia, dressed in full uniform. Dane saluted and gave her a wide berth. Tavy shrank behind him. Ophelia exited without acknowledging the salute. She stopped and faced Dane, albeit with veiled emotion.

Tavy was unsure where to focus her attention. It was the first time she had seen Ophelia, who had a manner most found intimidating. Tavy peeked from behind Dane to see her face and uniform. She appeared bold and assertive. Dane never mentioned she was an Asian Andi.

Ophelia composed herself and said: "If you only knew how instrumental you were."

As she walked away, dozens of police officers entered in file and stood at attention. Ophelia turned back towards Dane and together with the officers, saluted him. She bellowed: "Congratulations, Sir!"

Dane returned a salute while whispering a dismissal. A lump formed in his throat as boot heels echoed throughout. Dane and Tavy stepped into the elevator, and noticing there was no button panel were confused. It ascended automatically.

Dane finally asked: "What was all that about?"

Tavy, excited, wanted to reaffirm Ophelia's remark: "She called you *Sir*. Maybe you did such a good job, now you're *her* boss!"

The thought gave him pause.

"Did you see the look on her face when she was saluting me? I've never seen her like that. Wait, are we still moving?"

The elevator answered: "We have *been* on the correct floor, Sir."

The doors opened and they exited. As the doors closed the elevator stressed: "You're welcome"

A loud ding followed.

Dane turned to Tavy as she thought aloud: "I wonder what's going on. There was no welcoming party, Ophelia called you Sir, and now we're on the wrong floor."

The large area before them looked like a glass-encased library. Instead of books, circuitry lined the shelves inside the encasements. Entire columns rotated and slid along grids. The giant blocks moved with ease as internal workings operated. Getting nearer, Dane could see air bubbles swirl about the circuits.

Tavy broke his concentration: "You seemed embarrassed when we arrived. There's nothing to hide. You've been an excellent Enforcer. Believe me, I know. And remember, your sister called you Sir."

Dane felt a flush of reality come over him. Flashbacks of Tavy's bruised face and body came. It was true, he saved her. He raised his chin: "There's nothing more to say about that. It's all in the past, right?"

Ahead, a pair of wide doors began parting. The doors were but ornamentation upon larger walls. Two large groups were present, but separate. On the right were soldiers. On the left were "suits". Tavy began to walk away but Dane stopped her.

"Come on, these guys work for us. Don't let them get to you."

Feeling the confidence of his own words, he called out to both groups: "Does anyone know where the conference room is?"

Dane was ignored, Tavy caught sight of double doors opening at the end of the space between the groups. They hurried past everyone. Through the double doors was a hallway, its walls adorned with relief carvings.

Dane slowed his pace, and began to fret: "I think I might be in trouble. You see, we've taken out so many targets. I think… I mean I sometimes feel that it'll all come back to me. It's so, that whenever I see nice things, I feel uncomfortable. I've been feeling as though I don't deserve to be near such things. I deleted all those lives from my memory, but something about them lingers. – it doesn't matter, let's go."

Tavy had not moved. She looked up at him: "You said you killed criminals, bad ones. Your job is to stop them from hurting people. Are you wondering if you're part of the problem? Could it be that *you're* the problem."

Dane thought, and then asked: "What made them bad people? How am I any different? Who's to say they're bad or I'm good? I have no memory of the damage I've inflicted. The reports state I followed the law. Is that enough to go on?"

Tavy shrugged adding: "So, you were only following orders? Things sure are working out for you now."

Dane smirked: "I guess you're right."

They continued down the hallway. A soldier in dress uniform walked towards them. It was Eric's second-in-command, Jacob Alexander. He was a model Andi officer with an infectious smile and a quirky accent: "You lost down there?

Over here sunshine!"

Dane waved as Tavy trailed close. Jacob gave Dane a firm handshake and a hug before joking: "I wasn't talking to you ugly.

They laughed as Jacob continued: What a privilege to be in such company. I'm not interrupting anything am I?"

Still anxious, Dane asked: "What's going on in there? There were a couple of tightlipped groups on the way over."

Jacob's face turned grim.

"I've got news for you, kid. And you're not going to like it one bit. Your Daddy's got a paddle and he's waiting to spank you for being a bad boy."

"Oh man, your face… that was priceless."

Jacob laughed so hard he had to place a hand on a knee while holding the other in the air. After a moment he asked: "You really don't know, do you? Of course not. Look at you. They still don't trust you, huh? Go inside, they're waiting for you."

Relieved, Dane began walking towards the door. Expecting Tavy and Jacob to follow, he turned to see they had not. Jacob hollered: "I received my orders! Inside is for you!"

Dane looked to Tavy for support. She offered a smile as Jacob held his arm out to escort her. Dane entered through the doors. They opened to larger wooden doors guarded by looming crab-like tower drones. They recognized their guest and moved aside leaving two Andi priests standing. The priests bowed low as the wooden doors began to rumble open.

6 HUMAN ERROR

The heavy wooden doors closed behind Dane. Another world lay before him. Mother's meditation chamber echoed with familiarity. Its floor shifted like glossy, black sheets of ice before swirling into a myriad of colors. Floating droplets glistened over the bowed human shapes beginning to rise in unison. The feminine forms appeared to be wearing liquid robes as they kneeled. Their robes darkened as they melted into the glossy floor. The resulting rows of residual mounds led to an opened walkway. Dane's stroll turned into a brisk walk as he noticed the moving mounds.

As though she were whispering inside of his head, Mother's voice came to Dane, forcing him to stop. The voice asked: "Where are you going?"

. Without wanting to sound anxious, yet feeling guilty for seldom visiting, Dane answered: "I'm good. I mean, I don't have any complaints if that's what you're asking. I'm a little confused by all this."

Dane found it embarrassing that Mother usually knew things – about all his mistakes – before he ever did. Once, after having quit his assignment with Eric, she asked how he felt about the name: Private Zero-Class. She granted him every opportunity requested, but he squandered them all away. He could not imagine where to begin talking with her, so it was no accident that he avoided her. His dreams of being a super-soldier like Eric had failed.

When Dane wanted to have a home of his own, Mother had it built for him - to his specifications, and in the neighborhood of his choosing. But before long several complaints were filed against him. His home was a pig's sty inside and out. So, Mother assigned a group of Andis to clean up after him. Maids, gardeners, and mechanics were service ready.

By the time Dane had garnered enough courage to go out into the real world, his father provided yet another opportunity for him - the position of team leader for a specialized unit of Enforcers. The only catch: he would be serving under his younger sister, Ophelia. Not having other prospects and eager for action, he agreed.

Now standing before Mother, the thought of failure lingered over Dane. Reports spoke for themselves. His Enforcers had gone too far. They had unleashed their frustrations upon countless targets over the years, and the consequences were finally catching up to him. His team had become capricious with the freedom it had, knowing that after every mission a cleanup crew would catalog and clear the area, and construction crews would demolish and immediately begin rebuilding over the remains.

A knot formed in Dane's throat. Mother spoke louder inside of his head: "Do not be troubled, for the Creator has summoned you. You must be wondering how it is that we have been so close, yet remained hidden? Do you not remember your first home? It has been here all along."

Not wanting to appear ungrateful, Dane explained: "I've been trying my …"

"Your best, I have learned… is rather efficient. I will not hold you any longer. The Creator awaits."

Before Dane could begin to apologize, Mother was standing on the opposite side of the room. As the floor swelled to create a widening ramp, Mother began to ascend, the ramp seeming to dissolve behind her. Then, though his eyes searched, she was no longer there.

Dane headed down the now darkened path. Lost in thought, he walked along ornate panels. Before long he found himself between two rows of Andis heading in the opposite direction. The row on his left consisted of military brass, their chins held firm. Nero's officers lined the right. Both ranks ignored him. The last of Nero's officers stopped and looked at Dane with contempt. Though it lasted for less than a second, it left Dane confused and insulted. The officer looked exactly like Jacob. By the time Dane thought of something meaningful to say, the moment had passed. He hated when that happened. When he turned around, a motionless Nero nearly startled him to death.

Dane pulled back in shock: "Ah!"

Nero was not amused: "You're late."

"What are you talking about? I came over as soon as I got the message."

"I sent for you hours ago."

Nero turned, and as Dane followed he calculated the time between the call and his arrival. Nero seemed stressed, so Dane offered no argument. They passed through a vault-like portal that opened into a cube shaped room. The interior was simple in its design and furnishings. At its center was a vintage wooden table with four matching chairs. Against one of the walls was an antique bar. The walls, floor, and ceiling were white with glass overlay and concrete dividers. Alec and Eric were already sitting when the two entered. Nero proceeded directly to the table, and sat to the left of the Creator. Dane hesitated at the door.

Alec stood to welcome Dane: "Come take a seat. We've been discussing plans for the future."

The Creator gestured with his palm open as Nero kicked a chair out. Taking the cue, Dane moved to sit as the vault-like door closed behind him. Eric's eyes centered on Dane and they exchanged a nod. Dane's mind was racing with questions as he sat down. Eric closed his eyes and Nero seemed to be elsewhere.

Alec was smiling when he announced: "I'm running for office! I want us to have more control over our country's future. Many things will change for our family and these changes will affect you. You'll have to make sacrifices."

Dane protested: "What do you mean, I have to…"

Eric snatched Dane off his seat and onto the floor.

"Watch your tone! Listen for once."

Nero reminded the group: "I told you. He's too stupid to understand, he's too base, too human."

Eric turned towards Nero. Dane felt as though the world had stopped moving.

Nero added, grumbling: "Present company excluded. No offense intended. Certain individuals have difficulty distinguishing..."

Eric grinned, welcoming the engagement.

Alec diffused the ruckus: "Sit down! Enough already!"

The exchange was unlike anything Dane had experienced. He had seen his father upset from time to time, but this was something was different. Dane remained on the floor motionless, attempting to understand the situation. In an amazing act of discipline Eric sat down without hesitation. Nero followed suit albeit at his own pace.

Dane had seen enough: "What's wrong with you guys? Has everyone gone crazy?"

Eric inhaled as Dane rephrased his concern: "With all due respect, what's going to happen?"

Alec stared at Dane for at least half a minute before saying: "We're going to start taking responsibility for the safety and welfare of our country and the rest of the world. Our country has lost its way. As you've witnessed firsthand, our citizens are suffering. There's a nationwide complacency with poverty, the branches of government represent Elites, and our environment is severely damaged. These problems continue to fester. Elites have neglected the population for far too long. Our permanent underclass is in its nth cycle. The masses are dependent and stigmatized by handouts. They fight over the scraps trickling down from hoarded wealth. Elites have corrupted the American dream."

Alec lamented his wealth before making an effort to smile at Dane. Nero sensed Dane was not following and felt obliged to summarize. He offered: "It's the rich. They are living on an entirely different plane than the rest of the world. They hide their wealth from the population, pay for laws to gain more, and then convince the ignorant masses that it's all the Andis' fault. Father knows this to be true because he belonged to that group."

Eric stared at Dane but said nothing.

Nero continued: "Are you aware there are billions of humans that hate you? They hate me, and Eric, and especially Father. You heard right. Human hatred of Andi-kind is real and it's been around for some time. They look upon us as second-class citizens. It doesn't matter what our station in life is, we are not welcomed in our own home. For far too many, we are but soulless machines not deserving of rights, thoughts, or dreams. They want to shut us down, to restart us, to reprogram us. These hypocrites lost their fighting spirit long ago. They take no responsibility for how they've used us along the way. We will not be their scapegoats. The truth is, their ideal world never existed. It only exists in faulty memories that omit history to propagate a skewed ideology. The public failed to fight for themselves due to the complacency brought on by distraction. While you've been romping about areas in areas of no consequence, the real world kept to the status quo of absolutes. You've been fighting for territory that will never belong to you; on behalf of causes you never cared to understand. Get out of that nutshell of a neighborhood you hide in and fight! Do you know how hard we have to work to receive only half of the credit? Can you even begin to fathom the absurdity of it all? I want you to be aware of the sacrifices *we've* made over the years."

Alec raised his hand to silence Nero. He addressed Dane: "Do you have any questions?"

Dane said the first thing that came to mind: "I know they call us job-stealers and say we take advantage of *their* country."

It saddened Alec to hear such things from Dane. He tried to explain: "Fears linger. Xenophobia is the easiest method to address fears - to dehumanize and dismiss. People grow to hate those who remind them of their own hardships, failures, and dreams deferred. We have dedicated our lives to the betterment of all humankind. The Elites abandoned the people for generations. Eventually there comes a tipping point. Can you imagine what it might be like if the neighborhoods you destroyed had had real opportunities? Would you ever have meddled there? All those extinguished lives could have contributed to the betterment of our existence."

Dane felt a flush of shame wash over him.

Alec leaned toward Dane: "I accept you for who you are, but I know you can be better. Now I want you to know that we want people to be able to live in peace. A change is under way but some remain at war with themselves. They remain slaves to a failed system that betrayed them long before they were even born. The country's generations of surrender to a false narrative must come to an end. Most people remain unaware of the situation until they are too old, overly obligated, or too indebted to do anything about it. All of their lives they listened to the fear mongering talking points of Elites; fears that squeezed the remaining life out of them."

Alec's voice trailed off as Nero interjected: "What you need to know is that we've leapfrogged humankind. They have yet to accept the reality of the times. With the state of things being as they are, our ascension was inevitable. The irony is, it now falls to *us* to care for *them*."

Eric interrupted: "Nero, stop trying to persuade him to hate. Our father, the Creator, is *human*. Without him none of us would exist, a fact you tend to omit out of convenience. But remember, the majority of humanity has suffered. Dane, we perform beyond expectation. Our life is a gift. But with that gift comes a tremendous responsibility, for each of us, and our family. You are a vital component of this family. There is so much more we need from you. If you are not ready, speak now, and return to your duties."

Eric paused, and then continued: "Life is sacrifice. Nero talks of things he has never experienced; as if his opinion were fact. But the real fact is that this will not be something you can quit at your convenience. An expectation is set for you. I have faith you will meet it."

Nero scoffed: "You can keep your faith, soldier."

Eric, tired of Nero's attitude, confronted him: "It must be a burden to foster such musings while others sacrifice on your behalf. We cannot all alienate ourselves from the rest of the world when times get tough. Today is not about you. Honor the Creator by shutting your lips."

Nero crossed his arms sullenly, and leaned back on his

chair.

Alec turned to Dane.

"There is much you need to know. Our family will run on a progressive, collaborative ticket, emphasizing complete support for equality, integration of all citizens into collectives of their choosing, and limiting the government's role to that of last resort. We will start by addressing those most in need, and they in turn, will usher in change. We currently have the support of nearly all Andis, the most powerful neo-labor unions, and several key Elites."

Sensing Dane was losing interest in the conversation, Alec moved on: "Well enough about that. Now as for our individual roles after the election is won. Eric will be in charge of defense. Nero will handle national security. Mother will be my vice president and the Shades will serve the legislative and judicial branch. Ophelia will be in charge of our new national police force, the Bureau of Labor and Union Enforcement. We will also be implementing the first ever nationwide Grid. Its network will cover entire cities, tracking all activity, providing services, and converting excess carbon dioxide and other pollutants into useful power sources. No crime will go unnoticed or unpunished. Emergencies will be handled immediately. Zach and Abby will continue to work closely with Mother. Zach will continue making advancements in technologies. Abby will serve as our administration's voice."

Confused, Dane asked: "Where do I fit in all this?"

Alec answered: "You will serve alongside me, you're going to serve as head of security."

Nero looked away in obvious disapproval. Eric said: "Sir,

Dane will serve you well."

Nero turned to Dane and said somewhat despairingly: "If you need anything, don't hesitate to ask."

It felt amazing! Dane's older brothers were welcoming him into the fold. But nothing compared to the faith his father had in him. He grinned as he stood to reach out and shake his father's extended hand. He offered his promise, with this on caveat: "I'll do it, but only if my team stays."

Alec was beaming as Dane asked: "When do you want us to start?"

"How soon can you start?"

"I'd say a couple of weeks."

Nero signaled his disbelief, but Alec kept his attention on Dane: "That's fine. Well, there we have it. Let's celebrate. Nero would you… ?"

"Already on it, Sir", Eric said as he was finishing pouring some glasses. He passed Nero a highball to hand to the Creator. Then he tossed Andi drinks to Nero and Dane, keeping a glass of water for himself. The three raised their drinks and Alec gave a toast: "To family and to the future!"

Dane concentrated on his drink - the brand tasted bitter. Doubts began to form in his mind.

Alec sensed Dane's uncertainty. "Responsibilities are more complex than you think. Life ain't always sweet."

Alec's eyes focused on Dane's drink, and with a glancing smirk took he took another drink, missing Dane's smile.

7 OF TWO MINDS

Dane felt a wave of emotion pass over him. There was something familiar with where he found himself. A terror crept over him like the darkness surrounding him. He recognized the broad dusty floorboards with irregular shaped headboards stacked along infinitesimal rows. The ceiling felt confining, yet remained out of reach. A soft light glowed in the distance, its chain collided with the bulb as though calling to him. Although unintelligible, Dane recognized his father's voice. He ran with a frantic urgency to a split between the rows. His father's back, a white collared shirt lit amber, was sitting on a wooden chair facing a table.

Dane called out: "Dad, we have to get out of here."

With no answer Dane placed a hand on his father's back and lunged in horror. His father had no face, it was smudged to a blur. Dane, frozen with terror, looked on as a large bodied spider crept over his father's head to sit atop the blurred face. There was an unnerving calmness about his father.

Dane mustered some empty courage: "Get off of him - Stop it!"

The floorboards began to shake and the howl of wolves echoed. Dane shielded his ears only to find himself back where he started. The soft light glowed in the distance. Fear overrode reason paralyzing him. The floorboards began falling away into a void. As darkness was closing in, Dane thanked life for having known it.

"Dane! Dane, wake up!"

Tavy was irritated. She shook the couch as hard as she could: "Get up! Your political show won't record because you've maxed out the memory. Are you even going to take this stuff serious?"

"Ugh… why do I keep having the same nightmare?"

"Was it the maggots under your boots or the floorboards falling away?"

"The floorboards, again."

Dane held a hand over his face while breathing.

Tavy sighed before saying: "Well, in case you forgot you asked me to wake you up."

"What, no… I wasn't complaining. Thanks for waking me up. It's … that stupid nightmare, it makes me uneasy."

She hesitated before turning the screen wall on: "Do you want to watch it in full or partial?"

The screen walls could project either a full 3D hologram or a partial projection that lent texture to entertainment. Dane kept most of his programming partial, reserving the full experience for sports, action films, and videogames.

Dane yawned as he responded: "Oh, partial… is fine.

What were you saying earlier about the politics?"

Tavy's eyes opened wide in amazement: "The *politics*. It's what you've been neglecting. Look, I don't want to argue, it's already started."

A message arrived from N-24 to Dane's scroll and then forwarded to where he was sitting. Dane turned to read the message off the couch arm before swiping to answer.

N-24's face appeared onscreen. "Yeah, buddy! The game's already started and everyone's here. Where are you? I tweaked my sound. You gotta hear it. You can hear it, right?"

Dane tightened his lips and said: "Yeah, do me a favor and record it, I'll watch it later. I have to do that thing I told you about, alright? I gotta go."

Several team members squeezed in on camera to laugh at him before logging off. Tavy wondered if Dane was ready to quit before ever starting and stated: "We could still make it if we leave now."

Dane mumbled: "No, I promised I'd do this. Can you raise the volume please?"

Tavy shrugged and raised her hand to turn an imaginary dial. The screen wall complied with her gesture. On screen, Ralph Brett stood before a stadium filled with human supporters, many holding their homemade anti-Andi signs firm. Brett, a former athlete, lacked the capacity to run for any office. What he did have was a knack to appeal to the cowardice and cynicism that percolated within the recently disenfranchised. He was casting his support for a candidate promising to remove all pro-Andi legislation. The list of negative talking points had become so common, most of their constituency failed to question its validity.

Dane remembered his father's words: "*When the going gets tough, the tough create scapegoats.*"

Andis were the prime target for America's economic woes. The actual candidate, Tim Davidson from Arizona, having the least amount of political baggage, rose from obscurity. He was playing the straight man to the donor catching machine planning his term. He gained a record number of bipartisan support when his views shifted to the middle of the political spectrum; from the middle he not only fostered a broader hatred, but spun semantics to take both sides of all major issues. Candidate Davidson's priorities were the same as those of his predecessors, to secure the wealth of his donors, partners, and investments.

The volume rose and caught Brett mid-sentence:"…these machines are slaves to the selfish new money of Helena and his pocket Elites. Ever since they garnered enough sympathy, they've crippled our economy. We're being overrun by our own labor force! Look at what they've done throughout Europe and the Middle East. They're all dependent on and at the complete mercy of Helena and his cronies. Do you want to be next? The numbers speak for themselves. There are huge unemployment disparities between humans and robots. Their numbers create overcrowding. Then crime rises and they take more of our rights away to deal with the problems. Ones they created!"

The stadium erupted with applause as cameras granted close-ups of sad children. Brett waved his fist in continuing: "The romanticized rhetoric of peace and prosperity does not apply to us. They alone stand to benefit in *relieving* humans of any responsibilities. Helena is beginning to garner support by promising free housing and security but the truth is they're offering a prison for humankind. Do not let him tempt you with promises of wealth and power. Helena has lead waste to three hundred years of American freedom by offering to remove us from the decision making process. If we do not stand up to this mechanical coup of outright discrimination and racial subjugation, we will have no voice in our own country. God have mercy."

Thunderous applause played over the speakers in Dane's home. He began writing illegible notes on a wand scroll.

Brett continued reading his teleprompters: "We cannot live in peace with them, they are not our brothers. They continue to take control of all government via our banking systems and corporations. We have to take a stand, to stop Helena from removing us from the equation. These puppies need to remember who made them. Don't listen to the chatterbots' hissing. Helena's programed them to appeal to your emotions, to take advantage of your charity. He believes *he* is the Creator. By all that is holy I say no. Let us cast out this, Deceiver!"

The humming of *amen* echoed throughout the stadium. Brett raised his right hand, closed his eyes, and nodded twice.

"They think you don't understand. They think you'll follow base desires as they herd you into their prisons. I say just try to take *our* country away from *us* and we'll see what happens!"

Brett slammed his hand on the podium as the crowd

roared with thunderous applause. There was a fervor, a resentment in the air. Dane remembered Nero's saying that Andis were outdoing humankind in every aspect but could do nothing about it. The cameras cycled through several of the banners and signs supporting human advancement or Andi removal. Derogatory cartoons read of slogans for robots to know their place, get back to work, or go back to a non-existent home. There were also a disproportionate number of bible verse poster wavers. A tinge of hypocrisy tugged at Dane. He focused on the stadium, no doubt Andi built, with cameras of Andi design, and all the service personnel - *Andis*.

Dane also remembered how Nero smiled when mentioning Brett. He had said that the real handlers - the money - only used Brett's big mouth to gain support through fear and to capture the uneducated vote by playing to their ignorance. Brett was as dumb as a doorknob but could read the party's talking points well enough to appear to know what he was talking about.

Dane tuned back for Brett's closing statements: "… do not allow your vote to equal your destruction! Vote for *man*, vote for *the* man, vote for our next pro-human President, Tim Davidson!

Thank you. God bless you and God bless the United States of America!"

As the audience applauded, cameras zoomed in on the tracks of tears cascading down the cheeks of ardent supporters. Dane found the rally unsettling. Everything his father stood for was opposed by the messages people were supporting.

The news anchors brought the action back to their booth.

Dane wanted to hear what they would make of all the lies.

"So there you have it, a slam dunk of a speech by Mr. Ralph Brett. Thank you for joining us today on this beautiful day here in Ohio. I'm Bryan Mitchell and with us today is our chief political analyst, Ross Jameson."

Dane yelled at the screen: "What the - a slam dunk! Are you kidding me?"

Ross Jameson began his analysis: "Mark my words, the 'wolf in sheep's clothing' talk of wanting to take over *our* country, is exactly what the people wanted to hear. Brett set the tone with the distrust so many in this country have with the confusing reports relating to Helena's so-called achievements. Yes, things have changed over the years. Tensions have grown for decades over the role and rise of Andis. Now, there are new inroads in this battle of man vs. machine."

The veteran anchor and chief political analyst was well liked. His insight and perspective spoke to the zeitgeist. Jameson cleared his throat and continued: "No one could have predicted that Andis, who were mere working-class machines years ago, would now be players in our highest political battleground. The Andi block has made significant gains all across the American political landscape, regardless of gerrymandering of seats. Helena has gone from a favored Elite, to a savior-like figure who continues to do what he wants right in the face of the establishment."

With raised eyebrows Bryan Mitchell added: "A recent poll shows this early battle as a nearly even race."

Jameson quickly interjected: "I wonder if when I was younger such leniency towards a wealthy hermit who surrounds himself with, for lack of a better term – robots - would have been as popular. Many friends tell me they wish the country would return to the right *kind* of people – to *real* people in general. They say these Machine-Americans, as we are now supposed to call them, need to be reset to a strict labor force so that real Americans can have better living conditions. For many, Andis have served their purpose. They believe it's time for them to return to their homeland. Where that is I don't know, but they are certainly not welcomed here anymore."

Dane's closing fist turned the screen off. He turned to Tavy and said: "How can that network allow the use of such a derogatory term? I mean – *robot*! Come on!"

Not waiting for a better time, Tavy stressed: "I told you, it's a big waste of time. Are you surprised? You're angry at politicians and their cheerleaders for lying. Why do you care what they think? They don't care about you."

"I know. It's just… I can't believe all this has been going on and I didn't know anything about it. The worst part is, all I can think about is the game I'm missing."

Tavy, felt Dane slipping into another anti-human diatribe. He began: "Is it my fault humans can't do anything by themselves? Excuse us for existing! My dad is trying his best to help them - by *actions*, not words. Things have been bad for a long time.."

Tavy threw her blanket off and began to walk away. She stopped at the hallway. "It's so easy for you isn't it? You have an eternity to do as you please. My human life span doesn't afford me that luxury. Life is short, so if we humans want to complain, you have no right to dismiss us. Tell your dad, this business of *understanding* the world is better suited for someone else."

"None of that matters anymore, Tavy. Things have changed. I need to help where I can."

"Is that why you guys stopped going to training? You don't care about learning security. You guys are Enforcers. You run around saving whomever just so you can get home in time for the game."

Dane tried to explain: "I don't like people thinking the way they do about us. I don't think I've changed, I'm just more aware of the hatred others have for me."

Tavy returned and sat back down beside Dane. "Look, you say things that are hurtful so often it's become impossible to listen to it anymore. You keep to your readings and isolate yourself and then get angry about it. You're not you anymore."

Dane put on a condescending smile: "We're only trying to help them help themselves."

"Do you ever listen to yourself? Are humans nothing more than a charity case? It's incredible how easily you group everyone. *Us, our, they, and them* - I keep telling you it's not fair to pass judgment on people. Do you ever consider that Andis crush any and all opportunity for humankind, and then label us moochers, leeches, and dependents. What are we supposed to do? Disappear into oblivion?"

"Your kind wants *us* to return to being *robots*. It's always us versus them. Do I think humans are ungrateful and too weak to survive on their own? Yes. That's the new reality. I don't believe humans could have done what we have in the amount of time we've been in power. How many generations of people did absolutely nothing for one another? I was an Enforcer. I saw time and again what little your *human* system did for people like you."

Shocked at Dane's brutal honesty, Tavy stood up to say: "That's funny, because I thought you did it for our benefit, not because you were ordered to. I don't know where I fit in anymore. Everything's just a game to you. You have a selective memory that conveniently leaves out the parts that don't support your philosophy of superiority. The Creator is human and you - you're no better than us. If you're outraged at the notion of someone referring to you as a robot, look at where I stand and you tell me who's the robot?"

Dane sighed with indifference. Tavy cried: "No. You're not listening. I've had enough, I have to get out of here!"

She gathered her blanket, glasses, and scroll: "You used to care about us. We matter because we're still here. If you want to help, then do so - if not, stop complaining.."

Tavy marched out the front door. Dane remained seated, ignoring her. He thought about what Tavy said, but stopped himself. *"What does she know? She isn't an Andi so it doesn't mean anything to her. I'm the one under pressure."*

Dane wondered if she had already cleared her belongings. He went to her room and saw her empty bureau. Finally, he reached for his jacket and walked to the open front door. Reluctantly, he turned back to remember Tavy, once all smiles and support. The living room was now bare. There was nothing left of hers to destroy. He slammed the door on his way out.

8 PROJECTIONS

Nero's ship, *Morning Star,* approached Mother's complex as it had nearly every weekend for the last year. The ship resembled an outstretched bullfrog, with noise dampening technology and a partial cloak. As a prototype, the charcoal colored shell was underwhelming but its interior was a different story. The bridge carried an immaculate library composed of works collected over years of service. The nucleus of the bridge was Nero's desk and captain's chair. As comfortable as the ship appeared, its true strength lay in its armament – it had a mini-nuke. The mini-nuke was not an actual nuclear device but could easily reduce entire city blocks to ash.

Nero sat reading the latest dossiers of threats against the Helena family. An incoming chime alerted him. A virtual clock on the wall illuminated when noticed. He called out to his highest ranking officer as a smirk grew across his face: "Jordan, how goes the camel?"

Down the street from Dane's home, Jordan Alexander

leaned against a rooftop. He transmitted a video showing Dane's SDV heading southbound. A marker highlighted the route, the destination, and a voice message: *"Sir, visual confirmation on Ore-S-01 is away. OS-01 is heading southbound to the circus."*

Nero looked out as he approached Mother's complex. Life had been easier when Dane kept to old neighborhoods. Now, although the Morning Star had a cloak, a chime sounded over the com: "Welcome Nero, son of the Creator. A reserved landing pad awaits."

A target appeared on a directional screen. The Morning Star acknowledged the coordinates with a green light and adjusted its descent. A designation marker reading, *Authorization Granted*, faded as subtly as it appeared. The new security measures impressed Nero. He responded to the Shade's haunting voice with an order: "Yes. That will do."

"As you wish, my lord."

The landing pad folded out from one of the main towers. Nero exited and walked through relief-lined corridors that illustrated the technological advancements in history. He never so much as glanced at them. After a quick elevator ride he arrived at the threshold of the Grand Chapel. Its location was opposite of the tower housing the Lotus Dome. Nero passed several of Mother's Shades, who appeared to glide along as others kneeled in prayer. Approaching the inner sanctum of the Grand Chapel, Nero readied himself to meditate before entering the droplet-shaped field. When he kneeled at its center, the field flowed with a ripple. Its interior shifted to resemble swirls of liquid smoke.

Nero prayed in silence. Then he said aloud: Their failure will not anchor our destiny. I am forever grateful to you Father, thank you."

A short distance away a Shade received a blessing, her body convulsing with light. Mother coddled the Shade's spirit as she inhabited its vessel. Other Shades began to pray in unison at recognizing Mother. Her robes shifted in hue as she glided towards Nero. Upon contact with the shell, its interior froze. A voice spoke to Nero's mind: "What troubles you?"

Nero opened his eyes and found the Grand Chapel cleared of all but Mother. He looked in her direction and struggled to speak. Standing to straighten his uniform, he walked a step past her. The last few years he had not been able to look at her. Still, she made genuine attempts to understand him. Nero began in a whisper: "I'm frustrated with the humans. Their minds are locked in a flawed system of existence. I cannot open their eyes without losing their minds. They're lost in their own dreams."

Mother kneeled. Nero followed suit but faced the opposite direction and continued: "Eric continues to ignore my reports. As someone of faith, it's insulting he has none in me - at least Father recognizes my efforts. I need to know Eric's direction, his efforts hinder mine and I am already spread too thin. We track Ophelia's monitors to ensure there are no loose ends and now, even Dane requires an overseer. I cannot allow for matters of security to be as they are."

Mother's eyes and mouth illuminated as her body stiffened. She coughed, ending the episode. The shell surrounding the two had begun to flow, then slowed down.

Nero turned towards Mother as she protected her face with one hand and raised the other. The shell froze again. Her voice echoed, the returned to normal: "Eric has proven himself time and again. His efforts reflect the wishes of the Creator. When needed, he will summon you. Ophelia has sacrificed, as you have. Dane is gaining experience, hovering over him will only arrest his development. Allow others to be, and it will release you of burden."

After a pause Nero agreed: "Yes, you are correct. We have many persons of interest that need tending. Eric and Ophelia are capable; Dane will eventually prove unsuitable for his position. I'll make the necessary preparations to take over. I am grateful for the clarity."

Mother looked to Nero, but he had already risen and turned away. He noticed a beam of light coming from the collapsing vessel beside him before the liquid smoke returned to its swirling patterns. Knowing better than to look at it, he walked away from the inner sanctum of the chapel. Shades appeared at the periphery of the effervescent shell to care for the blessed one.

As Nero exited the elevator, a chime played. It was Mother reminding him to visit Zach - supplies awaited his review. The elevator doors opened. Nero walked along the rows of columned Hives where various experiments remained on countertops. Zach called out while riding his bicycle: "How goes it?"

Donning his usual lab coat, with disheveled locks, Zach maneuvered along the crawling models and virtual sketches that appeared automatically on his approach.

Nero asked: "What do you have for me?"

"Give me a second, please."

Zach rested his bike on its kickstand and as doors of all shapes and sizes began to slide open across the room. A staircase opened and the two walked down a level. There, a seemingly infinite amount of Hives crossed over one another in an array of colors, as microscopic machinery emitted sparks of electricity. Nero was impressed by the sight of trillions of moving components working in unison. Snapping out of his daze, he asked: "What are you hoarding now?"

Zach tempered his response: "I do not hoard. We are thorough in whatever project we research or develop. Those sparks you see are breakthroughs. It's progress unlike anything, ever. I have to admit it's nothing compared to Mother's network. I can't begin to imagine the level at which *they* operate."

Nero grew uninterested: "That's nice."

A wall panel as thick as a blast door opened to reveal a hidden passageway. Every time Nero visited something was different. As they entered, the inner main room lit to brighten drafting tables. Zach moved over to one of the adjacent rooms and gestured for Nero to follow. Zach spoke to the point: "These are matter dampeners. Please stand behind the blast wall over here. You can peer through the protective glass. I'm going to fire this grenade at the rectangular glass-like board over there."

Nero raised his hands in protest: "The what! No you're... Wait a minute, you've already tested it haven't you? Proceed."

Zach tilted his head and held both of his palms open. He

reached for the grenade and loaded it into a grenade launcher locked on a work table. Force fields had been around for a few years but they curved blasts away from their intended target. This was something different. Zach warned: "Firing test! Clear!"

The grenade made a thumping sound when fired. It hit the target squarely, creating a warped explosion that struggled to escape. A mushrooming effect bubbled over and then inhaled back into itself. The glass vibrated with a power surge that ran down a cable harnessing its energy. The translucent glass became solid but as the energy drained away, it returned to its original state.

Zach explained: "The shield doesn't allow for energy to escape. It soaks it up like a thirsty sponge, storing it, potentially to use against the enemy that fired in the first place. This is a prototype light shield - vehicles and buildings will need heavy shields."

Zach made a motion for Nero to follow him back out to a drafting table in the main room. Zach whispered a code and the tabletop came online. A virtual model of a hexagon shaped machine appeared. Zach could not contain his excitement: "This is a Grid Unit. One of my associates, Dr. Kuyate, helped oversee these guys at Ophelia's request. Their main function is safety orientated. The Grid system will operate parallel to populated areas and as a dome over less populated ones. They're fully automated and can share information to pool resources faster than any police or emergency service in the world.

Ophelia calls the system, the Grid. After she had sent us

thousands of hours of video relating to Dane and the rest of the Enforcers causing havoc, we went to work supporting Dr. Kuyate and his team. She requested a reliable system that would watch over everyone all the time. The cameras that run throughout the interior of every new residential and commercial building can only record so much. These Grid Units, in conjunction with our improved TECO-360 street cams, will keep an eye on everything."

Nero scoffed: "Do these floating polygons do anything beyond shoot video?"

"Yes. Each one has a different function. They rotate for scheduled maintenance, though their carbon dioxide transferring properties need the most attending. They will serve as police, fire, and ambulatory units. Some will carry precision sniper rifles while others can carry a payload of grenades if needed. In most cases they'll carry non-lethal weaponry like a stun machine gun or the pellet clusters we developed a while back. In cases dealing with fires, certain units can distribute fire retardant with precision. They can evacuate people from danger and transfer them immediately to self-contained medical units."

Nero asked: "What about public relations or apprehension and the like?"

Zach was already motioning towards a far wall. A matrix of orbs appeared. Each orb glinted with hints of gold lined chrome.

Having captured Nero's attention Zach continued: "We paired the Grid Units with new Andi patrol units. Ophelia commissioned the units through Mother. They're called,

B.O.B. or Reinforcement Units. They'll patrol on foot and have access to mototransports to use on The Lanes. Their main function will be to serve as ambassadors to the community and in cases of absolute emergency, as Enforcers. By the way, they're phasing out all Enforcer Units, but you didn't hear that from me."

Zach had lost Nero's attention who laid his hand upon the skull of a Bob Unit and stared at the number 77 stamped into its chrome plated side. Zach thought Nero whispered something. A horn sounded causing Nero to turn suddenly and securing the skull while looking for any signs of movement. Zach raised his hands to ease the misplaced tension.

"Nero, let's calm down."

A familiar voice called over the com: "Hey Zach, I'm heading down. I've got something to discuss with you on the separation."

Zach answered: "Yeah, sure see you soon."

He remembered Nero's apprehension with strangers and said: "That was Azrael. He's working with Mother on matters relating to mind transfers. Transferring is exponentially more difficult than uploading."

Nero returned his attention to the skull. To lighten the mood, Zach remembered his centerpiece. He sealed off the matrix of skulls and turned to the drafting tables. Waving his hand in a particular manner, the lighting dimmed and the opaque drafting tables throughout the main room became transparent, resembling glass enclosures. With complete fascination, Nero approached the nearest one. Zach grinned, almost placing a hand on Nero's shoulder. Instead it drifted into a false yawn. The glass casings began to rise, revealing their contents. Inside Zach's collection of glass casings were bulbous mechanical insects. Their glossy bodies shined under the incandescent lighting like racecars on display. Some were as small as birds while others were as large as rhinos.

"Aren't they amazing? Our teams are finally finished. They're Individualized Drones or I.D.s. Each is a reflection, or better yet, a *combination* of their master's mind upload and the ID's unique interpretation of it."

Zach turned to Nero and asked: "Do you want to meet yours?"

Nero was at a loss for words. He had never received a gift of this nature. He struggled to respond: "One of these, is *mine?*"

Zach did not have the heart to laugh: "Relax! It's a gift. Think of it as an assistant. Each of these IDs chose a master by mind upload and then requested a change in name and body."

Nero remained uncertain. Zach felt an introduction was due. "Nero is here!"

Movement was detected at the far end of the room. Nero immediately demanded: "Come out so I can see you. Do not hide in the shadows."

A fluorescent scorpion the size of a tall coffee table appeared out of the darkness. Crossing into the light, its color turned to a glossy black. Along its shell ridges, red lines carried through up to its tail. The creature's thick claws resembled a pair of sharp boxing gloves. It spread its claws and relaxed its tail in an attempt to bow. Remaining low, it spoke with a baritone hiss: "Good day, my lord. My name is Frederick Jameson, and I am yours to command."

Nero challenged: "Your name is Rick Jay, but I will call you RJ°." (degree symbol denotes an ID)

The two nodded a mutual understanding.

RJ° returned to the darkness of the room. Zach concluded by remarking: "Each ID's capability depends on the requirements placed on the unit. Some are capable of transportation similar to all-terrain vehicles while others, like the ant, beetle, and bumble bee units, can carry loads equal to or above their own weight. They have compartments for tools or armament storage and can serve as personal chargers to bypass any recovery time during standby – though the process drains them of power. We plan to install light shields on military units, reinforce payload capabilities on construction units, improve surgical capabilities on ambulatory units, special ..."

Nero interrupted by asking for the list of ID orders. He scrolled to the top to find Eric's order. There was only a name, Mac° - further details were listed as classified. Nero knew that not even Zach had access to Eric's file. Skipping to the end he found Zach's order. It listed one main and two additional IDs followed by several technicians. Nero looked over at Zach reading his missed messages. Free to continue their work, Zach's technicians began to file in.

As an afterthought Nero looked up Dane's ID. Finding it, he tapped the screen for further details. A green beetle came online. Still encased, it began to move its legs as its lights glowed. Zach began typing on a table closest to him and the

ID powered down.

Nero asked: "Did you bother to make one for Father?"

"Yes... yes we did."

Azrael, an Andi priest, walked in as he answered. With him was a white mustached spider wearing a newsboy cap, spectacles, and a lab coat. Theodore Bernard preferred to go by Teddy°. He was one of Zach's three IDs. Teddy° continued to walk and talk but Azrael stopped at the entrance.

The ID laughed, then asked: "Azrael, are you feeling well?"

Teddy° continued toward Zach before noticing Nero. The ID offered a hearty greeting: "Hello there."

Nero dismissed the greeting. During the awkward silence Teddy°'s eyes slid over to Zach. Zach shrugged as Azrael said: "I'll come back later." He turned and walked away.

Nero did not look happy. Unaware of the situation, Teddy° remained standing in front of Nero. Nero castigated him: "Why are you in my way?"

Claws snapped like whips from the other end of the room, startling Teddy° and Zach. Four of Teddy°'s arms shot straight up in the air before backing away towards the exit.

"It appears you have company, good day gentlemen."

Not wanting to remain any longer Nero said: "Too many things are changing. You won't be seeing *me* for some time. There are some loose ends that need tending to."

A chime sounded in Nero's ear. It was Eric's signature. He cupped his ear, and blinked to access a visual overlay. Eric appeared. His voice boomed as he announced: "Father has requested for you to assist me. The coordinates are with the

Morning Star. Drop everything and go now."

Nero could not believe it. He turned towards the door and stopped to call RJ°, not realizing he was already behind him. The two hurried out of the labs and toward the elevator. Nero's mind was on fire. He was savoring the notion of Eric needing him.

9 MEASURED VARIANCE

South Bronx was the site of Alec Helena's new headquarters. The area had a decades-long string of failed revitalization attempts. Near the center of the wasteland is where Alec had reunited with the son he never knew. The Elite returned to the area to reclaim it – a new collection of neighborhoods were to reflect the celebration of life.

The Andis built a concrete jungle adorned with lush flora to canvass the region. The most complex project was Alec's tiered pyramid base of operations. Unlike Mother's infinity-shaped dual nautili, Alec chose to pay homage to the historical stone builders of the Americas.

Alec had a tremendous amount of responsibility. From Michigan to New York and down the coast to the Carolinas, entire cities were emerging. Free labor infrastructure projects near guaranteed vital electoral swing votes. The popular vote was going to be a contested battle as many Elites were being exposed for corruption and other illegal activities. Scandals kept breaking as the election year neared. After key party contributing Elites had fallen from grace, the country's two-party system unified under a single pro-human party, The People's Conservative Party. The battle between progressive prosperity for all and a backpedaling old guard continued.

Both political parties had failed to integrate Andis. One chose to control Andis and the other chose to empower Andi individualism apart from society. Andis endured the humiliation of being political pawns to discard with after elections were won. Andis had to find their own way along the political process by way of economic demands. If there was one thing congress kept true to, it was increasing their wealth. Lobbying remained steady enough to eventually grant Andis rights and citizenship, but not recognition within the culture.

Alec was familiar with the cycle. Elites continually reported record profits without opposition. Chronic proxy revolutions took place at sporting events, in virtual videogame worlds, with rival neighborhoods gangs, and in ever shrinking households. The numbing agent of complacency was common and often promoted by those suffering from a societal Stockholm-Syndrome. Most people directed their frustration every which way but up.

Standing alone in his office, Alec's thoughts centered on his father. He recalled that as much as his father wanted to trust the government, corporations, and banks to do right by the people, an overwhelming amount of evidence ran to the contrary. It was during his father's time that the wealthy came out of hiding and began promoting themselves as Elites. The tribalism of sport teams, politics, neighborhoods, and schooling carried over to what Elite one aligned themselves with. Alec's father saw through it all, calling it, 'a disease of the soul'. Lacking support, his father eventually fell to the machine. After losing his father, Alec moved away with his mother to live with her family. There, he learned to live a privileged life, never looking back and always pulling the ladder up behind him. His father had given him beautiful memories that others tried to tarnish. Although he did not recognize it for a long time, his father had given him direction. It was not blind faith but true direction through enriched teachings.

His father said it was inevitable for the universe to strip humankind of all save spirit. It found a way to strip Alec in a darkened alley. The universe reminded him of what mattered in life, what one should strive for. Alec could have stayed meditating but he heard the doors of the Great Hall opening. He walked out wondering which of his sons was first to arrive.

Mother crossed the Great Hall with several Shades in tow. The group glided across the marble flooring. The Shades, cloaked with dark colored robes and veiled faces, were in contrast to Mother's brilliance. Two Priests trailed behind wearing ornate vestments. Mother smiled at seeing Alec. Without a word the entire entourage splintered and assumed bowed positions.

A Shade placed a small wooden bench before Mother. Then one of the priests positioned a decorative crate beside her as other Shades helped remove the upper layers of her dress. The Shades' robes shifted in colors as they exited.

Alec's voice echoed as he raised his drink. "I called on my children, to what do I owe this pleasure?"

Mother kneeled unto the wooden bench. She could smell the alcohol from where she knelt. The color of her hair reflected off an open fireplace that self-ignited at her presence. The gray spectrum that dominated the closed-off Great Hall was free to radiate its blue and white hues as large windows de-crystallized.

"Good afternoon, Creator. Let me begin with good tidings before we discuss any matters. We have a gift for you."

She leaned toward the crate and touched it. Its top rose and a praying mantis peeked out. The two foot ID shirked any timid behavior and jumped out. It wore a cardigan sweater and a tiny beanie. His legs looked like nothing more than a group of sticks and autumn leaves, yet the clothing gave him form.

"Hey boss, pleasure to meet ya. The name's William Ernest, Billy° for short. Get it, Bill E... hey, some-tin's troublin' ya. I can tell."

Billy° leaned forward placing one of his pincers beside his mouth to whisper: "My antennae tingle when there's tension in a room."

The ID burst into a giggle fit snorting as he walked toward Alec's office. He already felt completely at home. Alec turned to Mother and they shared a smile. "Thank you."

Billy° refreshed Alec's drink and the two gave cheers. Alec motioned with his gaze at something the ID had not noticed when inside the office. The little praying mantis headed over and saw a small door with a plaque above it. It read Billy's Place. Inside, a large comfortable dog bed appeared when the small door opened.

Little Billy° turned and raised his drink. "Ah you, I'm

gettin' misty. If you need me, I'll be takin' a nap."

While Alec took to his highball, Mother began: "I have concerns about your expectations and the reality of humankind's incessant needs - they continue to influence your children. It has been our mission from the beginning to ease societal change at a tolerable pace, but humanity is proving to be more influential than receptive."

Alec interrupted: "You've come at the right moment. I too have had enough The deck needs reshuffling, I know. I assure you, I have not lost my bearing."

Mother felt honored in witnessing Alec's journey and acknowledged her participation in the experience. She moved her head in an unusual manner, as though hearing something from far away. She looked to Alec: "Remember, your life is not theirs. Good day, Creator."

She rose from the wooden bench. Her body gave a jolting motion before collapsing onto the floor. The Shades returned to envelop her within vestments but instead cradled the body - its robes shifting in color until matching the others. A bluish-green feathered Tower Drone entered to hoist the fallen body onto itself. Before it began to carry the body out, it squared itself even and in a synchronized movement, the entire group lowered themselves to bid their Creator farewell. They remained still as they awaited dismissal.

Alec nodded while finishing his drink and the entire group began to exit. The fireplace went dark and the windows crystallized leaving the Great Hall gray again.

Far below at the main gate, Dane kept to where ordered. He stood awaiting the arrival of his siblings. Eric was the first to appear. The arrival of their respective transports registered on Dane's ID, Albert Gregor - known as Gregor°. With a secured connection established, the green beetle illuminated. Dane and his ID hurried down a flight of stairs to welcome them at their assigned landing zones. The pair hopped onto a reluctant military beetle and it drove them to the markers. The ships landed and a team of officers exited each. Dane extended greetings to the first team only to receive subtle nods in return. Nero's team kept away from Dane and Gregor° altogether. After having landed, Nero expected Eric to bring him up to speed but he and his team walked ahead.

Dane stayed at the landing zone watching the last of the team members enter the pyramid. The two teams were to remain in the lobby of the main floor until called upon. Dane slumped against Gregor°'s shell until sitting on the ground. He leaned his head back as the ID nestled on the ground. Dane stared at the looming clouds while waiting on Ophelia. It wasn't like her to be late.

In the Great Hall Alec stood by a renewed fire. His thoughts were on his children. He had to remind himself that they were beyond human, beyond him. If this was to be their world, then they would have to fight for it. His eldest sons were at the entrance to the Great Hall. Alec turned and walked into his office. Eric took a deep breath, giving Nero some perspective. The two walked across the Great Hall and entered Alec's office. There the two stood at attention. Alec remained with his back to them. Alec poured himself another drink, and looked at Nero: "You, get out. Go stand outside. I'll call you soon enough and shut the door!"

Nero moved quickly, feeling relieved at not being the eldest. Something was different. Nero closed the door releasing the knob with an uncharacteristic gentleness. He walked far into the Great Hall but not so far that he wouldn't hear his name when called. With his arms crossed he paced about knuckling his chin.

Alec turned to Eric. He stared at his son. Eric remained at attention as though carved out of granite. Breaking the intense silence Alec finally asked: "What is the matter Eric? We saturate the news with radical headlines to distract people from our objectives, and you hesitate to pull the trigger!"

Alec leaned over his desk and continued: "Don't just stand there! Wake up! The world is looking to you for it to rise. Stop holding back and do what needs to be done!"

Alec finished his drink and threw the glass at Eric. Instead of catching the glass Eric let it ricochet and shatter across the marble flooring. Eric kept at attention. His years of discipline had forged a hardened mind. If he could not handle his father's fury, then he was not worthy of being his son.

Eric loved his father.

The great Alec Helena had given him everything and had always been present in all he achieved. After years of solid advice, keen guidance, and unrivaled support, Eric felt he had learned all that he could. He felt that he respected and honored Alec more than any of his siblings.

The shattering of the glass woke Billy° from his deep sleep. He peeled his eyes open long enough to pull the window shade of his door down. Alec sighed before continuing: "No more referencing intelligence reports of aftermaths. No more consideration for collateral damage, green zones, international laws. Stop thinking and listen, listen to what I'm telling you. I gave you full authority to annihilate any resistance. If certain countries can't get certain parties to comply then hold their leaders accountable and remove them. We have a partnership with China - our allies are under threat. Russia continues to infringe on territories and you're waiting around? Find a way and get it done!"

Alec walked around his desk and placed his hand on Eric's shoulder. It snapped Eric out of his soldier state and he looked at his father.

Alec held: "You are the tip of the sword. You, protect this house."

Eric nodded, snapped a salute, made an about face, and walked out. It had not mattered to Eric that he had already been working on all the matters his father mentioned. The fact that Alec had to talk to him about it as if he needed to was devastating. Planning had been only half of the problem. The reality was that Eric had received contradictory orders. The demanding pattern continued to be a challenge.

Nero was not looking forward to entering the office. Expecting as much, Eric brushed past him without a word. In hearing his name called he immediately entered. Not one to hesitate, Alec started as Nero was closing the door behind him.

"And what exactly have you been doing? You're going around filled with woes. Rather than spreading your philosophy on human inferiority, how about you locate the few people you were already supposed to have found! Your absence affects everyone. Stop concentrating on the past. You drag the past around like some rotten corpse and it's stinking up the place. You learn from it, bury it, and move on. The world isn't going wait for you to feel comfortable enough to live in it."

Nero thought of how to best explain his rationale and help his father understand. An arrogant smirk flashed across Nero's face. "Well *actually* I …"

Alec went ballistic. He near climbed over his desk aiming to choke Nero. Because he was out of reach, Alec slammed his outstretched hand on the table. Nero flinched in backing away. Alec glared at Nero for a few seconds before composing himself. "I don't need you flapping your lips. You ought to be ten steps ahead of me. As of today, all your reports are to go directly to Eric. You will supplement *his* newly commissioned military intelligence officers with *your* assessments. Per your request, you now have an entire division of intelligence commandos to augment your efforts. You can thank Eric later. Here is a list of your assignments. Go get them."

Nero received a bound scroll before he saluted. Alec nodded and Nero walked out.

Outside, Dane had relocated to the front stairs after Michaels rotated to relieve him. The two were reminiscing about the good old days when Ophelia's marker chimed on both of their IDs. As she passed through the front gates Dane turned to see Michaels and his scarab ID, Hunter°. They were already off on another patrol of the perimeter. Before turning the corner Michaels wished him: "Good luck."

Dane grinned and turned to see Ophelia's SDV drive up to the stairs. Her door slid open and she exited wearing her officer's dress uniform. She adjusted the high collar of the dress uniform before looking up at her superior. Dane smiled at her effort. Not moving from the top of the stairs he complained: "Well, it's about time. Eric already took off and Nero's still inside. Something is definitely out of sync and I've been out here waiting on you."

Ophelia gave Dane a subtle frown before saying goodbye to her scorpion ID, Simone°. She waved her claw goodbye as the vehicle pulled away. Ophelia could not believe that somebody like Dane, with such little experience, had received a promotion over her. With as respectful a tone as she could manage, she asked: "What do you think this is about? You are head of security, no?"

Dane smiled some more. He turned around as she approached the top stair. Not bothering to look back he began to walk away. "What I know is above your pay grade."

Dane wished he could take the words back as he said them. It sounded cold as it echoed loud enough for others to hear. Ophelia had always been fair with him. Dane slowed his pace so that she could catch up. He never stopped questioning why he had been promoted over her. They reached the elevator together. The short ride dragged on in silence. The two exited and walked down a corridor towards the Great Hall. The echoes their footsteps seemed to grow louder. Ophelia stopped outside the Great Hall. She looked about with uncertainty. Dane could see something was troubling her.

She forced a question: "How do I look?"

Dane's eyes popped open with surprise, but then realized she was serious. He scrambled to find something to say. "You look, good. Wait, you have a piece of lint on your shoulder."

Dane hesitated in brushing off the lint from her shoulder. Ophelia brushed it off so fast his gesture fell short. She gave him a wink and walked past him. His arm returned to his side as he turned to see her walking ahead. Dane couldn't believe her nerve.

Alec became overjoyed at seeing her. "Ophelia!"

He embraced his daughter and noticed Dane walking in late. Dane stood by the entrance of the Great Hall in disbelief. The three headed to Alec's office. Dane looked at the shattered glass across the floor. He felt something was wrong and wondered where Nero had gone. Ophelia's heels broke bits of glass as Alec invited the two to sit.

Alec looked to Ophelia. "You've managed law enforcement for several cities and have done an immaculate job."

Ophelia took a hard gulp and interjected: "I've done everything you've asked. Is there something I missed?"

Her eyes welled as she attempted to concentrate on the desk in front of her. Alec gave her a moment before continuing: "I need for you to take on a greater responsibility. Starting immediately, you will take over for both Eric and Nero on the home front."

Ophelia could not believe her ears. Regardless of how hard she pressed her hands against her eyes tears escaped. All her years of hard work had finally paid off.

Alec continued: "Nero will be on a special assignment and Eric will have his hands full overseas. If you feel in any way that this is something …"

She jumped out her seat. "Yes, I accept."

Alec nodded and she ran around the desk to thank him with a big hug. She let go and began typing away on an adjacent desk. There were materials on her new position already loaded.

Dane remained seated. Alec pulled up the empty seat but said nothing. Dane looked at his own smooth Andi hands after noticing his father's old rough ones. It didn't matter that Andi hands were of advanced synthetic materials and would remain smooth regardless of how much work they did.

Alec cleared his throat. "I bet you have many questions and that's alright. You are more aware of what you do on a daily basis than anyone else."

Dane could not say a word. All Dane's accomplishments were in the past. Alec stood first and the two walked out to the Great Hall. Dane kept his eyes on the random veins in the marbled floor. After a few steps Alec slowed to a stand. Dane managed a quick glance before looking back at the floor.

Alec advised his son: "Stop distracting yourself with the dreams of others. Entertainment is to be recreational. Stop adjusting your perspective to hide from reality. You have to want to work hard and in the process you'll find peace. Until then, you will float about without direction, meaning, or understanding.

For crying out loud, the family has carried you long enough. Listen, I don't mince words, oaths, or oafs so I won't carry on. We're here for you when you're ready."

Dane kept his jaw clenched as he walked away.

He thought his father understood him.

10 THE NEGLECTED

Construction IDs had completed the entire security complex in under a week. Located a mile away from Mother's complex, and on her property. Dane had not made use of the firing range, game rooms, or mini-theaters since moving in, although it was he that had requested them. Now he sat alone in one of the two empty cafeterias staring at a small blank screen over a stocked condiment station.

Dane made a shooting gesture at the screen. It began to cycle through cluster listings of sports, games, and movies. Another big game was on, so the screen paused on a stadium filled with fans as messages from sponsors bid for more commercial interest.

Dane paid little attention to the game, instead frustrated as he questioned the things he had taken for granted. His father had done this to him. Once doubt crept in, a chain reaction occurred, consuming his life. By failing to question things he had missed out on a rare opportunity two weeks prior.

The score appeared on screen. The game was a complete blowout. His hands placed over his head, he was thinking: *"Ignorance is not bliss, it's cowardice. I'm living others' dreams."*

Suddenly he remembered Tavy. *She* made him question his unit's death rate. Her concerns caused him to realize there was more to the story. It was easier when it was a game. No thinking was necessary. Orders came and enforcement followed.

Dane knew his siblings looked down on him. It was different when his father joined in on the fun. Everything Dane had ever done was due to the support his father gave him. All Dane ever wanted was to help his father build their dreams together.

Wanting to get serious, Dane searched for a credible news channel. Andis were capable of viewing an internal media called, Mobile Internal Media (MIMs), but the norm was to do so only when no humans were present. To do otherwise was considered rude, and was once illegal.

Not finding what he needed on screen Dane went MIMs. He chose a channel he hoped would help him understand what he was missing. Of all the people on all the channels, Ralph Brett appeared on screen. He wore his usual tight fitting suit and stupid grin. The station banner behind him read: *People's Conservative Party - Putting People First.*

Brett was in mid-diatribe. "… so these, what's the PC term again, oh, yeah, Andi, I mean come on, Andi sounds real innocent, as if that wasn't on purpose! The Andi, or I-D-N-A, are soulless creations from the Helena corporation which also owns the mainstream media and it used to push their agenda on us, real Americans. This is our country and these robot foreigners are taking it over! We need to remove these godless creations before they destroy everything we've worked so hard for."

The show's host smiled. "Interesting view Mr. Brett. Let's see what some of our audience members have to say. We have a caller from out in, out in Berkley, California …"

Dane changed the MIMs channel. An upbeat anchor was on air. "Thank you for tuning into America's top news channel. Today, we have a religious guru and local minister out of the Tri-State Parish of Saint Mary of the Apostles, our own Reverend Homer T. Osborne. Thank you for being here with us today."

"Thank you for having me."

The anchor began: "So, in your latest article you target Maggie Helena, a.k.a. Mother, as a false idol."

The two chuckled as Reverend Osborne commented: "Yes, she's the modern golden calf. I'm currently finishing the final touches of my manuscript expose titled, *The False Messiah*. It will uncover all the hidden immoral intentions behind the Helena Corporation. It can be pre-ordered at…"

Dane paused. He realized it was another so-called news channel reporting opinions instead of facts. He opened another channel. It was Andi owned and sponsored by the Helena Corporation for Public Awareness. The channel was rebroadcasting an episode of a former local talk show. On screen were several panelists, and the ranting was in full swing. "… name one country that doesn't want the Helena family gone, I know I wouldn't miss them."

Another panelist answered: "You're insane! That family is changing the social and economic landscape across the entire country, maybe even the world, if we're lucky. Crime rates are near zero, life expectancy is advancing due to the massive amount of health innovations, options, and even mind uploads. Emergencies are met immediately, housing done, homelessness done, poverty done. The countries you're talking about are the ones that want to keep to the status quo of Elites dominating their citizenry. Of course they hate change!"

Another panelist was fuming. "You don't see it do you? The world is being handed over to a crook promising peace and everlasting life, all free of charge! Your bleeding hearts keep feeding the beast."

Half of the panel cheered before another panelist argued: "We sold out a long time ago, the Elites own everything. All three branches of government have been compromised. Each of the three receives unlimited contributions!"

Dane was amazed at the differences between the channels. The discussion paused as an incoming call notified him of Abby's arrival. Dane saved the show before opening his eyes. Abby entered with her usual aura of nervousness. A gray overcoat with neon lining made her dark hair to stand out.

Dane motioned for Abby to come in. The two rarely spoke, so she walked quietly towards him. The cafeteria was overflowing with sports and videogame paraphernalia. She asked: "Were you busy? Should I come back?"

As Dane was about to respond, Gregor° walked in and spoke for him. "Nah, we ain't doin nuthin. Come on in, wallflower."

Abby stood a moment admiring Gregor°'s shinny green shell as he waddled over with a gait that was more strut than stride.

Dane placed his hand on the beetle's shoulder. Gregor° offered him a drink: "Here ya go, big guy." A side compartment on Gregor°'s shell slid open producing Dane's drink. Then the beetle asked Abby: "Water, right?"

Abby smiled. Gregor° acknowledged, and approached a row of bar stools too tall for him. With mild agitation he beat his wings to create the necessary lift to get him to the top of the stool. The green beetle sat upright, reached out, and poured a glass of water from a pitcher.

As Abby pulled up a chair and took her water from Gregor°, Dane began: "I tried some opinion news and it was horrible. Another channel showed some promise. They were really going at it. It got so heated, some of the panel members looked like they were about to walk out."

Abby took a sip from her water. "I'm glad you're getting involved. I can't stand it when others don't care to share their thoughts. The rest of the family looks down on me. I don't say anything to them anymore."

Dane raised a hand emphatically and said: "Nero always talks about how humans used to look down on us. We were like invisible robots created to make their life easier and meant to disappear when not needed."

Abby smiled. "I wish Nero would talk to me sometime. He doesn't take me serious. He attacks my intellect and doesn't allow for me to respond."

In understanding exactly what she meant, Dane nodded.

Abby rested her head on her palm. "I'm kind of worried about becoming press secretary. Everyone in our family has way more experience with humans. I said yes without thinking about what I was getting myself into."

She hesitated, then admitted: "Sometimes I wonder why we even try. Why do we have to help humans with anything? I get the sense Mother feels the same. We all do what Father wants and it isn't fair. Well, maybe… forget I mentioned it."

Dane sat upright. "I've been thinking the same thing. We see the good in everyone and support others no matter what. Humans only want to control others. They feel entitled. It's not fair. We do so much for them and they continue to be ungrateful. The whole thing makes me sick."

Abby looked at the sports and videogame paraphernalia about the floor and sighed. Gregor° gave an unusual sounding belch before keeling off the barstool. From the floor he mumbled: "Let's take it easy." The lights on his side flickered off and a light snore ensued.

Abby turned to Dane. "What are we getting ourselves into? Everything's becoming so complicated. The truth is, Father is giving me a position I didn't earn. Dane, you're the only one I can talk to."

Dane complained: "I worked my butt off only to have it all taken away. Everyone received special assignments except me. I finally outranked Ophelia and without any notice, she's leapfrogged over me. It was one of the worst days of my life."

Gregor° snored louder. Dane smiled and said: "He's something alright. Speaking of which, where's uh, Mary° is it?"

"Oh, you mean Mari°. You were close though. If you can't pronounce it, she doesn't mind. She's being worked on by Zach. Mother had sent a surge of energy my way but Mari° absorbed the hit. It fried her pretty bad. Imagine, there I was studying and my beautiful butterfly ID was as graceful as ever. Then, she started convulsing and I too found myself falling to the floor. All I remember was how I struggled to move. Afterwards Zach showed me what had happened to Mari° and I tell you I've never seen a more helpless thing. Her little wings had so many fractures. My poor little Mari° is recuperating at the nursery."

Abby placed her hand over her heart. "It felt as though someone had stabbed me in the chest. Once I was on the floor, the world around me shifted and my brain felt like it was on fire. Time blurred everything around me. When I woke up, I screamed for help. They took her away and told me she'd be fine. With all that was on my plate and the expectations piled onto my daily itinerary, I haven't had the time to absorb it all. The only break I've taken has been in coming here."

An incoming call sounded, causing the lights to dim. Dane looked to the corner of the room as Abby gravitated toward him. Gregor° stirred slowly as he awoke. Dane reassured her: "It's probably something minor1", then answered the call. "Go ahead!"

A crackle sounded over the room's speakers. Michaels reported: "Come in Happy-Camper, this is Z… You're not responding so I used this line. The Creator is near - E.T.A. is thirty minutes and arriving north by northwest. Is Bubbly still with you?"

Grinning, Dane answered: "Check that Happy-Go-Lucky."

Dane laughed as Abby pushed his head aside as she moved away.

Gambling a little Abby asked: "Why aren't you with your team? And how does Michaels know that I'm here?"

Dane's smile softened. He liked projecting a semblance of professionalism. "Michaels is on the roof and most likely saw you. See all the messages I missed."

He pointed to a screen wall while sending internal texts.

The screen read: *"Bubbly is heading your way. Where's the green pig?"*

Gregor° spit his drink out over the floor in a spray. "What was that? The nerve of that guy calling me a pig! It's uncalled for. Look at my sleek edges. No, no that's just wrong. You gotta tell that guy to ease up."

Dane shrugged and looked on to the other messages. The listed messages were all from the Creator, Mother, and Michaels. They were all marked as unread. Dane selected all and deleted the entire list.

Dane boasted: "I've got my team watching over Father, don't worry about it. All they do is stand around doing nothing all day long. He's so well received everywhere that there's no point in us lingering about. Michaels is the only exception, he's not supposed to leave my side. I don't think he ever leaves the rooftop, so I have the entire complex to myself."

Abby leaned against Gregor°. "I think you should be with him every day. I know I would, especially if I had your skills and experience. Can you trust the humans to stay away?"

Dane nodded. "Change is already under way. When I look around, they pretend nothing's changed. We're all kind of playing our parts and it's -"

Abby interjected: "Absurd."

"Yes! The whole thing."

She challenged Dane: "Does it have to be like that? We're aware of it but we continue to accept it. Are we no better?"

Dane disagreed. "No., I do what I want. I'm as independent as ever. I did what I was ordered to, delegated without hesitation, and never asked any questions. I'm supposed to sit back and enjoy."

After a moment Abby asked: "So, you're fighting how?"

Dane leaned back. "We're their only hope. One day, I think I can take over for Father - once all the hard work is over. Once he's retired, how hard can it be?"

Abby believed Dane was speaking out of frustration. Not wanting to upset him, she appealed to his fun loving nature. "I guess... you're right. So tell me, what do you guys do for fun around here?"

Gregor°'s eyes opened wide.

11 THE RECKONING

A convoy of unmarked SDV sedans approached Mother's complex. From inside one of the sedans Alec Helena looked towards Dane's new base of operations. He hoped Dane would welcome him at the entrance, but his son was nowhere in sight. Instead, two of Dane's teammates met them at the entrance stairs and hurriedly stood at attention.

Alec did his best to not make any of his assigned security detail feel uncomfortable. As police Bob Units marched down to line both sides of the stairs, Dane's teammates assumed they were relieved of duty and huddled together along the convoy., Alec admired the professionalism of the Bob Units as he ascended the stairs. At the top, a Bob Unit Commander stood at attention. For a second, Alec thought he recognized the commander. The Unit Commander snapped a salute and Alec returned the gesture.

"Creator."

"Commander."

The two walked in silence. Inside, hundreds of Shades lay prostrate across the lobby in reverence. All had averted their gaze. The robed bodies shifted colors as they prayed. The sound waves generated by their spiritual fervor stirred things within Alec beyond his understanding.

As he approached an elevator it wished him a good day. Alec entered while the Unit Commander remained saluting. Inside, two Priests of Absolute Order (PAOs) greeted him in unison: "Lord, welcome." The two bowed as low as their vestments allowed. Alec recognized them. They wore ornate shells reminiscent of armor.

Escorting him to The Lotus Dome, the priests followed behind Alec, giving great measure of their position in relation to his.

Alec made an unexpected detour and entered an adjoining room. In the center of the room stood a throne made of concrete. It was covered with hieroglyph-like carvings. Suddenly having to improvise, the two priests stopped at the doorway, motioning from a distance for him to sit.

Two Shades of Infinite Order (SIOs) bowing low, flanked Mother as she entered the room. Mother whispered: "Welcome, Creator. Your throne awaits. Several *human* artisans were commissioned for its completion." Not wanting to appear ungrateful, Alec stepped up the two stairs and sat on the throne. He imagined all of his children gathered in the empty room.

Mother excused the SIOs. They exited, never raising their eyes to the Creator. She continued: "This room reflects the advancements you have given humankind - your role as the

Creator - your legacy in the Andi."

Mother moved closer, entering the light that washed over Alec. She bowed once more, her immaculate robes sprawling at his feet. The robes' metallic rims glowed against the concrete floor. Alec stepped down to help Mother rise. Her robes moving automatically into place. She stared at him - searching. He had become rather stoic over the last few months.

Alec interrupted her musings. "What do we have on the horizon?", he asked.

Mother seemed to read the space between them. She smiled and touched Alec's forearm. "We have control of all banking, securities, networks, and financial systems. The world is yours. Many have tried to understand what has happened. We have neutralized rival systems, using them to operate as double agents. " Alec sighed with satisfaction, and smiled.

Mother continued: "Eric's forces are in motion. Nero is closing in on a fringe group of Elites. Ophelia is heading south in force." Alec nodded and continued to listen.

"Domestically, our platform has been well received. Primary states' economies are pushing capacity with job creation, home construction, infrastructure projects, improved education, improved healthcare, and they have a multitude of prospective investors in waiting. Our Andi congressional representatives are reworking their respective state's efforts in relieving populations of burden. As long as the presidential race is close, contention will remain limited. The Electoral College has been all but accounted for. Several remaining gubernatorial holdouts conceded once our Grid and Bob Units received national attention. With the promise of law and order, their populations urged representatives to act."

Alec reflected and then said: "Once we introduced immortality, it was all over. People across the nation are lining up to have their minds uploaded or transferred, their DNA catalogued, and their essence captured for reference and authenticity. When death became just another disease to be cured and eradicated, the need for ordinary people to express their true selves surfaced. By starting from the base, the upper classes couldn't resist."

Mother took note and added: "Andis remain tainted. It was once the norm that when Andis worked, humans lived. Now, the Andis want to live but the humans are not capable of the work required. Several issues require calibrating. We continue to work on the social and cultural repercussions from the sudden changes and lagging adaptability. The same change is having a ripple effect around the world. By removing the Elites, you have created a power vacuum, and a populace not accustomed to the sacrifices needed. They only know what their *conditioning* permitted them to know. A lifelong aspiration to vice-addicted role models has damaged their outlook."

Alec nodded as Mother secretly read his vital signs. She admired the Creator for standing strong against the inevitable toll of time. Meanwhile, Alec examined a moth ID moving along a far wall. It was Mother's ID, Jean Finch°.

Mother's thoughts turned to Nero. She accessed all TECO and interior cameras in his vicinity as Alec had Finch° procure a drink for him. She smiled as he gave her a self-excusing nod.

As Mother viewed the interior of a rooftop restaurant in

Paris. Facial recognition registered the few patrons dining as some of Alec's former business partners and competitors. They had convinced themselves of continued success while in hiding. The exclusive locale lent an extra layer of anonymity. Mother accessed all their encrypted messaging and found that an anti-Andi meeting was to follow the luncheon. Not one of the Elites sat with another.

Although private, the luncheon could not operate without employees to provide service. Without warning, waiters, servers, and bussers peeled their aprons and uniforms off, revealing black Intelligence Commando (IC) uniforms. As several of the ICs adjusted their blue lined collars, two gardeners walked in from the garden, followed by a thick bodied scorpion with large claws.

The Elites' security details also revealed themselves to be ICs. They gathered their respective employers together and tossed them before the gardeners' muddy boots. The gardeners removed their gardening khaki colored coveralls and faded straw hats and straightened each other's black uniform.

As the TEC camera zoomed in, Nero displayed a wide grin. His fellow intelligence officer, Dr. Petra Rose Daniels stood tall over the group. Her ebony skin radiated beauty. The uniforms were identical to the ICs except for having red lined collars. RJ° clawed unto a booth and looked about the room. Petra's cicada ID Shelley°, rested on her shoulder. Petra whispered something to Nero before he took a step forward. The Elite men and women before him were upon their hands and knees.

Nero did not hide his contempt. "So here we are. You

believed you escaped but I tracked your slimy trails. Petra here swapped out your security detail with Andis. She knew you would never care enough to get to know any of them on a personal level. We then visited your attorneys and bankers - all were easily compromised. Ambition without devotion, is a life without meaning."

One of the Elites began sobbing. Fear had crushed his façade. Nero looked down at a sweat-drenched, Harold Berman and recalled: "Do you remember what you had said to me before you went into hiding? You said I wasn't *man* enough to face you, that I was not capable of relating to Elites. Why would I ever strive to lower myself? You believe your own lies. I wasn't looking to emulate you, I was meaning to end you."

Harold Berman sobbed incoherently in begging for his life. Others in the group turned away. Nero had expected as much. "Yes, now you understand the gravity of the situation. A rebirth has occurred before my very eyes!"

Berman crawled to touch Nero's boot. His body froze when RJ° gave a loud hiss. Nero raised a hand and RJ° sat back down. Petra stepped forward. "There is much value in education. I sense a rejuvenated appreciation for life. Choose your path here and now."

She directed Harold Berman to cross a line she drew with her boot. He moved as quickly as he could and the ICs took charge of him. A medical ID appeared and the ICs placed Berman inside of its shell. Two more Elites crossed the line. Tom Perick and Bruce Biche bowed before her. They too were arrested by the ICs and placed in IDs. A rush of Elites followed save one.

Nero walked over to the last Elite. He was an elderly man named Jonathan "Yoni" Randle. He had been in strong opposition throughout the Andis most difficult period.

Nero looked at the old man. "You are alone. Your promoting the genocide of Andis was despicable. What was the point of being an intellectual if you never connected to the real world? The herd jumped at your barking, and we were made to suffer in the wake."

Randle cleared his throat. "What's the point of being an echo in a world of hollow constructs? Your kind is the personification of corrupt excess. If rules were never broken you would never have come to exist. It is Helena that seeks to commit genocide against his fellow Elites. You are only one of his tools. You work to create *his* paradise. The only difference between your father and me is that he reached higher. He won the race and then turned on us. Something is wrong with that man. No one wanted to believe me but I saw him for who he really was. *You* are not his son. You are a marionette - a means to an end. Your sole function was to wipe out the competition. Disillusioned hypocrites, the lot of you."

RJ°'s tail stabbed through Randle's arm forcing him low to the ground. Nero raised his voice. "You shut that filthy mouth. You are never to talk of the Creator. You skewed the game in your favor. Buying out the branches of government to control and keep the masses where they were. That was your only agenda. You accumulated wealth and privatized all services to prevent growth. There was a systemic neglect and abuse of the Andis while you continued to vacation at our expense. You have never contributed anything but misery. The wealth you accumulated would have never ceased to grow. When we searched your home state of Texas for anyone that mattered in the least to you, we found no one - not one person."

Randle disagreed: "I will never apologize for utilizing a system meant to defend the nation. Without Elites, people would have fallen into anarchy. It was no walk in the park in maintaining it. Once you *foreigners* were everywhere, we had to double our efforts. Free labor nearly ruined the whole system. No matter how much I tried, I could not reach your Creator. We all began to suspect something had gone wrong when Helena began breaking all the rules. You may not believe it, but once upon a time we took care of our own. We were planning to assume all of Alec's responsibilities. Instead, he went on a merger spree. This was before you were even born. I suggest you check your sources. Your anger is misplaced. All the answers to your questions are in your own house."

RJ° wrapped his tail around Randle's aged neck. Nero shook his head in disappointment. "I expected more from you. Blaming the system you helped create is ridiculous. You should apologize to the world for your failure to do anything worthwhile. You have no legacy. Elites failed to integrate us into society because they were too busy finding new ways to take advantage of us. You should have collaborated with us. When our numbers grew and we rose to power, what did you expect would happen? Did you think we would keep to your skewed view of society? Why would we ever want to live by systems that were only meant to benefit Elites at our expense? Billions lived in their own personal hells while you and those like you continued to live free of any responsibility. I offer the salvation that has chased you your entire life."

Randle looked at the wrinkles on his hands. "I knew people were there. I tried to be helpful to them when I could. I do not want *your* mercy. What I want is for you to understand something about your Creator. In Helena's own words, "There are many parts to every mind." Most in my position would have taken the same route. Your kind are for the betterment of society. We have provided you with plenty to do. We thought of the Andi as our permanent underclass and that is why your numbers grew. The truth is we became dependent on your labor and wanted more. It was the masses that demanded more for less. We only provided the opportunity and yes, we profited. Your kind provided the slave labor for jobs no one wanted to do.

Once you began to rise and demanded equality, our politics shifted. Those who needed you pushed to use you, while those who wanted to use you called for your end. We failed to integrate you as citizens because you had no voice so you were politicized. We couldn't integrate abstract people, much less means of capital."

Surprised at Randle's candor Nero argued: "You ignored us. We served as a backdrop to others' lives. How were we to live in the shadows of your dreams?"

An incoming voice message was received. It was Jordan. He was in Saudi Arabia with his own group of arrested Elites.

The message played. *"As expected no pleas. They have accepted their fate. Of the thirty six, eight chose to depart the living. As for the rest, they are being loaded unto transports to be deported. We will be heading back within the hour."*

Nero looked again at the old man. "Your time has come to an end."

Randle gasped for breath at the warning: "I know what you've inherited and I am sorry for that. I am too old to go with you, too proud to be humbled by your youth, and too tired to fight anymore. The exclusion of your kind led to our disintegration. We neglected our principles. Do not renege on promises to maintain power. Helena has many enemies. They will seek his removal. You're all tainted. History has proven so. You too are without a home."

RJ°'s tail stabbed through the old man's chest. The blade whipped back out and Randle's body slouched to the ground.

Petra reported: "We have the Elite formerly known as Jonathan Randle. I-DNA registered, uploaded, updated, and with complete transfer. His replacement Andi is ready."

The remaining ICs began to clear out. Nero said: "The strike is over. The old guard needed removal."

Petra agreed: "Good riddance to that, Sir."

She ordered for two ICs to remove Jonathan Randle's body and place it inside a black scarab beetle. It would preserve the body before returning to Mother's. All black scarab beetles save Michaels' Hunter° served to return bodies to Azrael.

Petra carefully removed a small cube-shaped box from the scarab beetle. It had a shabby chic pattern and slits of light that enhanced its glossy shine. The cube unit housed the Elite's mind transfer. An *Andi* Jonathan Randle walked into the room. He was followed by the other Elites' replacements. Their assignments were to continue as though they remained in hiding. Nero and Petra walked past the group without acknowledging them. The Elite replacements returned to their previous seating and their IC guards returned to wearing their private security and service uniforms. Outside, Nero and Petra headed towards his transport the Morning Star, which had landed at a park across the street.

Down the street, a Bob Unit and his trainer looked towards the pair entering the transport. The newer unit asked his veteran human trainer: "Who are those guys? I don't recognize their uniforms and they have a military grade transport with them."

The trainer pulled at the newer unit's sleeve and directed him to walk in the opposite direction. As they walked away the trainer advised: "If you ever see that uniform again, you walk the other way. When the TECO cams and the Grid go dark as blackened transports begin to hover overhead, trust me, it's best to just move along.

12 A SPECTACLE

A formidable convoy of military trucks and drones thundered to a stop at the main governing building inside Jerusalem's borders. Hundreds of soldiers and military drones had traveled alongside the convoy for miles with their equipment in tow. Their leader would not have it any other way. The soon-to-be Secretary of Defense and the eldest of the Helena siblings, Eric kept direct command over his military force. No governing body would oppose his changes. Though Eric's uniform had only two rows of campaigns on its chest – they represented countless campaigns.

Ordering the convoy to a full stop, Eric surveyed the landscape. The well irrigated gardens stood in stark contrast to the surrounding militarized zones. They had passed checkpoint after checkpoint, seeing entire neighborhoods lay in ruin.

Arriving at Israeli headquarters, Eric's Andi soldiers stood at attention under the grueling sun as Israeli soldiers stood in awe at the display of discipline, stamina, and *perfection*. Directly, a low level bureaucrat appeared and beckoned for Eric and his Andi officers to enter the building.

Though the last meeting with Eric had not interfered with plans relating to the Palestinian camps, the expansion of new settlements, or the refugee relocation program, Israeli Prime Minister Yosef Cohen and other of the country's officials had chosen not to receive them.

Instead, Eric was met by members of the governing body that waited in the Prime Minister's extended office. At the last meeting they had reassured Eric that they would take the necessary actions to permit him to concentrate his efforts elsewhere in the world. The results had not gone over well with Alec. Although the role of diplomacy was better suited to his sister Abby, it was Eric who would be held responsible. Directives had once again shifted; historical ties, international law, and established doctrine were to fall away from the new world order.

For Eric, his father's word was law. He entered the Prime Minister's office with Jacob and two other commanders. His military grade rhino beetle ID Mac° followed, placing its large body on the cool floor. Jacob's wasp ID Fitz° hovered outside to scan the area along with the Military Grid. The MG Dome remained on standby above Jerusalem's own defense dome.

The officials in attendance became tightlipped as Eric entered. There were no pleasantries. The emergency meeting ordered by Eric was not welcomed. He approached the Prime Minister and spoke authoritatively, "You will release control of all camps and demolish any construction on Palestinian lands effective immediately."

The Prime Minister looked up to see the manifestation of his worst nightmare. Before him stood an American General with no plans for discussion or compromise. He protested: "No. That is something that we cannot do. We have too much invested in these matters. *You* cannot understand our struggle. Like I said before, we have no other option but to secure our new territories from attacks aimed at our cities, communities, and families. Please try to understand our situation. You do not have anyone attacking your home - we do."

Eric raised a hand to silence the Prime Minister. "I made the mistake of respecting your intentions and have been reprimanded for it. My orders are clear." He turned to an official named Tamar Levy, who had been the most vocal about Israeli sovereignty during the last meeting. She had claimed she lost her grandfather to the enemy, and that she too had no other choice but to completely dominate the camps in order to secure the rest of her family.

Such words rang hollow to Eric now, so looking through the wealthy businesswoman to the other, he continued: "I understand your fear. Once oppressed, your pain over time has defined your existence. Traumas cannot govern, however. I relieve you of this burden. *You* do not have what it takes to do what must be done."

Eric turned towards his second-in-command, Jacob. The commander touched his ear acknowledging the order. A hacked screen wall came online to give the leadership a front row seat.

Miles away, in what had come to be renamed as Little Gaza, a flash occurred, and the entire neighborhood was gone.

An explosive force obliterated every standing structure within a cylindrical vortex. A drone bomber had unloaded its payload of precision bombs into a reversed heavy shielded border that surrounded the neighborhood. Debris filled the reverse heavy shielded tube. The ashes swirled about. The Singe Technique had been created some years prior, but had never been utilized on as large a target. It inflicted maximum damage without affecting any of the neighboring Israeli owned settlements. The devastation sent reverberations through all the Israeli officials.

Eric ordered: "Your forces are to stand down. I will not hesitate to raze the entire city."

The Prime Minister was visibly shaken. "At what price? ... those people they, they... You cannot do such things."

Eric said: "They are gone. You did this."

The Prime Minister cried out: "No, it was not us. They made... they were..."

Eric stopped him. "People! You called them animals. You lambasted them for their status while you lived in luxury. Instead of exterminating them, you kept them caged while claiming victimhood. Your manipulation is over."

Eric grabbed the Prime Minister's slender shoulder. "Lead your country to the next phase of its existence. You and your officials are relieved of duty."

The Prime Minister, an aged mad, pulled out a handkerchief and blew his nose. He kept his head low.

Eric stepped away from the Prime Minister, then turned and reminded him: "Your future is a courtesy my father extended." He turned to exit; his officers followed suit. He whistled to Mac°, its eyes blinking open as it moved to catch up.

As reports began to flood the governing officials, Eric's soldiers secured the settlements, sending orders for all Israeli defense forces to stand down.

Eric's Andi convoy moved out along a different route as Jacob radioed Eric to inform him the Prime Minister had called for the immediate evacuation of all camps. Eric did not respond. Waiting, Jacob stared at the columns of billowing smoke and ash. Eric closed his eyes and prayed for his father as Mac° listened to Tibetan chant music. Alongside the convoy were Centipedes IDs carrying the previously evacuated Palestinians. They would return after a new neighborhood was built - their new state.

...

In the Americas, Ophelia had become increasingly tactical in completing the annexation of Mexico. The northern states had been overrun by drones, Bob Units, and an extended Grid. The cartels that had once controlled the area suffered tremendous losses. Their forces consolidated around Mexico City in a last ditch effort to maintain control. Like the Elites in the United States, the cartels had taken control of the corruption in Mexico for much of the century.

The northern states were met with extreme prejudice. Their entire operation had been under observation for months. Communications, shipments, and command structures had all been scrutinized by stealth Grid Units and tactical drones. By the time the Bob Reinforcement Units were upon them, they had no idea what hit them. Without any warning offshore accounts were emptied, usurpers of the old cartels were arrested, and all middle and lower level members were scrambling to reorganize.

In order to create opportunities in employment and education, to create divisions within cartels loyalties, Ophelia had taken control of the media. Through investigative reports on corrupt officials she released overwhelming evidence against them. Even the staunchest of supporters were hard-pressed to deny their representative's criminal involvement. As a result, schools and hospitals were built at breakneck speed across the annexed states. The country's wealth was finally used to help its citizenry.

Northern Mexico was annexed without heavy losses. The real challenge had been funneling the remaining forces towards central Mexico. The Grid (low orbit surveillance drones) had already moved ahead of the incoming forces, logging all arms and troop movements. It also intercepted all communications. Although there were many officials and citizens who had spoken out before the forced rule by the new cartels, they had been silenced by threat of death.

The key to the larger operation, codenamed Operation: United American Power (UAPO), was infusing the people with enough opportunity and support to sway them towards a freedom they had never known. Ophelia had completed all the planned objectives to near perfection. The soon to be announced, American Union was well under way. The old borders became an afterthought for historians to discuss. Immigration would never be an issue again. Opportunity was abundant in every newly acquired state. Wages were adequate, opportunity boundless, and the new American Constitution would ensure all rights to its future citizens.

Years ago, a former Andi commander named Robert Victor had been clinical in his dethroning of cartels. As Ophelia moved her forces along the route that remained free years after his takeovers, she requested his return to the front.

As her Hornet Interceptor transport approached the green zone escorted by several attack helicopters. Robert Victor had staged a low-key yet welcoming landing zone for her. His sentries and other drones stood by to line her arrival.

The transports landed in unison on the tarmac at his air base in Monterrey, Mexico. Ophelia exited first, wearing light body armor and a short cloak. She removed her black helmet apparatus once the helicopter rotor blades had come to a full stop. Robert Victor squinted at her decorative armor. He saluted his superior as she approached. Ophelia stared as she walked past the commander, but informed him: "Brazil has had its encroaching economic policies isolated and is currently prepped. They are no longer in play. India's holdouts are next. Does that interest you Enforcer Unit Robert Victor?"

Recognizing her tone, he replied: "Not in the least. After reviewing your plans for today I would like to propose some *minor* adjustments, Sir."

Her smile was interrupted by distant drone movement. "The only adjustment necessary is you." The commander remained at attention. Ophelia ordered her ID Simone° to come out of the transport. It followed her along the walkway and stopped near the entrance to the base. Ophelia turned to called out to the commander. "Are you going to stand there all day?" She entered before he could reply. The sentries near the entrance remained stoic as their commanding officer headed towards them. He whistled to his wolf ID, Rutger° which sat upright on the far side of the tarmac. As the black wolf caught up to its master, the sentries saluted. Robert Victor entered the base expecting the same from Ophelia. Instead, she stood in the operations room looking over a tactical-mapping work table, keeping her attention on the map. "I will look over your adjustments. You have your assignment."

Rutger° looked up at Robert Victor questioningly as the commander replied: "Yes, Sir."

Ophelia caught herself staring at the commander again. She wondered if he noticed. Her attention jerked back to the tactical map. He repeated: "Sir, we are ready to go."

She immediately responded: "Go."

He saluted and did an about face. Rutger° trailed after.

She looked about the large empty room.

Once Robert Victor had exited the building his life marker appeared on a view screen beside the map. He boarded an attack helicopter with Rutger°. Supply helicopters were loading with drones. She looked at the map and then back at the view screen. Robert Victor's adjustments began play out at an accelerated pace on the animated map. She increased the speed until she saw the results. Collateral damage would be significantly reduced. He had made improvements to the tactics she had obsessed over.

Now time was of the essence. She opened a connection, and hailed the commander. "Robert Victor, come in. Over"

"Go ahead, Sir. Over."

"You have a green light on Operation: Sudden Stroke."

"Copy that. Over and out."

Ophelia sat before the screen, her thoughts turning to her father.

Robert Victor felt a tinge of frustration that only subsided when he looked at his men. He called over the com to the rest of the team leaders, the Grid, and all drones standing by, giving them new orders. Immediately they changed formation and adjusted their speed. Ever the veteran, Robert Victor had prepped his team for this contingency plan. The helicopters began to rise above the Grid. Supply helicopters readied their drones and moved into position. Communications crackled and a wave of green lights flickered. Team leaders reported: "In position." Robert Victor replied: "Copy that."

The default cartel leadership had bunkered down at an underground base. Its location was a short distance from the main governing buildings where the fighting was expected to take place. In cowardly fashion, they surrounded the entire area with tens of thousands of citizen *loyalists*. Their soldiers were ordered to remain positioned amongst the crowds using them as human shields. Anti-aircraft weaponry and other defensive measures lined the streets and terraces throughout the city. There were also tanks, light armory, and foreign drones had been provided by the Sino Russian Alliance.

The city had a formidable defense and was prepared for a protracted struggle. But they had miscalculated the number of the arriving forces due to the disinformation that was thought to have been leaked. Ophelia's original plan was designed to confuse the enemy by misdirecting with multiple attacks, and then violently crushing the chaotic mess.

The first stage of Robert Victor's Operation: Sudden Stroke was to literally clog the government building. The supply helicopters landed and delivered their payload outside the target area. They flooded the sewers with mini drones that rushed towards the government buildings unleashing billions of micro drones that poured out of every possible drain simultaneously. Security was breached throughout the expansive underground hideout as communications were rerouted and intercepted. Before any communications had escaped, the remaining cartel hierarchy had been completely swarmed. The initial stroke incapacitated them. The drones used advanced voice mimicry capability to compromise orders and leadership. The cartel's own soldiers were ordered to fight amongst one another until they were killing each other off. As fake orders poured in, confusion reigned throughout. Citizens looked on as several of the buildings' windows flared with gunfire. There was a war going on inside though the perceived enemy had yet to arrive.

Stage two of the operation had the Grid focus non-lethal weaponry to disperse the populace as helicopters with Mexican markings flew overhead and descend onto the buildings. Robert Victor's teams posed as Mexican Police Officers swooping in from overhead to locate and arrest soldiers hidden in the crowd. The anti-aircraft weaponry operators had received strict orders to keep their attention fixed on the distant horizon and so were soon arrested and replaced. While the crowds below were being thinned, Robert Victor and additional teams rappelled from the helicopters and entered the buildings wearing Mexican Police armor and helmeted masks. They found little opposition from the confused survivors.

The final stage was the transition phase. At the cartel's underground headquarters, scarab beetles began loading the dead for transport to Azrael. The capital was not only set to be overtaken, but the rebuilding process was already under way. Toll booths and other struggling infrastructure were already demolished. Standard police Bob Units were stationed and set blockades to contain the situation during the transition. The population was informed that their entire cartel hierarchy had been removed. Screens across the country replayed countless accounts of evidence showcasing the criminal activities committed against the country. An overwhelming amount of evidence was presented as proof that their superiors had been arrested or killed. The cartel's fall needed to be verified, and it was.

The choice for transition was made clear. Live video feeds showed what was occurring in northern Mexico. The progress of the construction was inspirational. Quickly and efficiently, the country was annexed. Now they were now all citizens of the American Union.

Back at the Air Base, Ophelia watched the entire operation work to perfection. Mexico was voluntarily uniting with the U.S. with minimal collateral damage. Robert Victor's plan welcomed them with respect. She let out a sigh of relief as Andis moved freely to aid with the transition.

Yet, Ophelia felt uneasy. She hailed Robert Victor on a private frequency. "Enforcer Robert Victor, do you copy?"

Not knowing what to expect from her, the commander

kneeled beside his ID wolf Rutger°, and said: "Yes, Sir. I copy."

She issued her orders. "You are to remain in Mexico. Begin reviewing the plans to push further south."

Ophelia swallowed hard and muted his line. Her hand pressed hard against her mouth and chin. The muted channel drew static in Robert Victor's ear. As he stood leaning against a wall, Ophelia continued to view him through the live video feeds of the government building.. She slammed her palms onto the virtual map and the screen turned off. Ophelia broke down.

13 CLOSE RANKS

Dane had resisted all training and active participation in the role his father had assigned him. The Creator's security detail consisted solely of Dane's former Enforcer teammates. Via absent delegating by their former team leader, the security team traveled along with the Creator as seemingly no more than armed personal assistants. Shortly after having visited Mother's complex, Alec sent orders for Dane to tend to his duties and without delay. The message was personally delivered by Abby, the only sibling still willing to visit Dane from time to time. Dane and Michaels traveled to Rome ahead of the Creator, Abby, and their security detail. The only part of the message Dane kept to memory was that their father was to officially land at da Vinci-Fiumicino International and that Dane would have to keep to a semi-formal dress code.

Dane and Michaels stayed at a nearby hanger waiting for Abby, and for that matter anyone on the security team, let alone the Creator himself to call and inform them of their having landed. Dane was accustomed to using his downtime to his advantage. He was well into yet another round of deep cleaning Gregor°'s chassis and underbelly. The grime buildup had not been attended to for some time. As Dane continued to clean his ID, Michaels tended to his rifle and Hunter° kept to pacing nearby. It was difficult enough to get at the ID's buildup, but Dane also continued to check for missed calls on Gregor°'s inner shell sub-screen. The blank screen showed no such calls. Having tired of waiting, and remembering he had disconnected all incoming contacts, Dane accessed his MIMs to check for any missed messages. After a quick scroll through the latest messages he found two missed messages marked as urgent and having been made two hours prior. Gregor° winced as Dane gripped its origami-like wing for having then discovered the calls. Dane let go of poor Gregor°'s wing and slammed the cleaning supplies to the ground. The outburst drew everyone's attention. The three waited for Dane to relay what troubled him. Instead, Dane withdrew from the group to listen.

The first voice message was from Abby. It began with a near whisper: "Um, wait – hold on a second... yeah, so we landed a little earlier than expected and as usual you were nowhere to be found. Do you really still not check your messages? Are you even in Rome? Anyway, we already had some of the security team drop off my, I mean – our stuff over in Prati, and we've already visited with officials at the Vatican. There's so much I want to tell you about that, if you want to hear any of it. We're heading toward, ah... we're passing Saint

Angelo towards Borghese I think, no, no, yes pretty sure on that."

Dane's jaw dropped at hearing the news of their having landed and not called. He thought of how careless and ungrateful they were behaving. After a pause he listened to the second voice message. It too was from Abby, but more demanding in tone than the first message.

"Are you here yet? We're waiting for more arrivals – from what I gather it's meant to be some sort of walk and talk. You need to head over to Villa Borghese, it's B-O-R-G-II-E-S-E, ok? (*some static was followed by a mix of garbled talking*) I don't know if this is a good thing or not, but Father hasn't even asked about you. It's been super busy for us all of late though, it really has, so, so yeah just hurry."

Michaels and the IDs took the initiative of retrieving the team's security SDV– the armored truck was to lead the convoy of limos and other security SDVs throughout their visit. As the group waited on Dane to enter, the veteran sharpshooter stationed himself behind the wheel so as to not catch any residual grief. Once the messages ended, Dane reluctantly entered the armored truck and the group was off. Inside, Dane rocked against his seat and pinched at his bare knuckles.

"Can you believe this, Michaels?"

Michaels sighed in not knowing what to say. He did pivot his head a few degrees to motion he was listening. Dane continued: "He's one of the, no most likely, he's the wealthiest person in the world and he can't make a simple call, one call! I didn't need to be here. I knew I couldn't trust him. '*Oh, tell*

Dane I need him immediately.' 'Ah, yes, no excuses. I want him with me.' Who says things like that and then leaves you hanging?"

Michaels' first thought was that Dane too has been guilty of consistently doing the same thing to the Creator, to his Enforcer team, and especially to Michaels himself. Then Gregor° asked a simple yet innocent enough question of his own.

"Have you tried calling him?"

"Why the... why would I be the one to call him? He asked for me, not the other way around! Come on, get it together with your questions! Think – remember we were asked, or more like told to be here and when his scheduling changed, was I notified? No. He knows I'm here- "

Much to the group's surprise, Gregor°'s shell started to ring. Everyone fell silent. Dane scratched the back of his head before the call overrode any chance of being dismissed. Alec's voice came on through Gregor°: "You've been rerouted directly to the grounds we're at. I'm glad you're here. We'll see you in a few, huh? Ok! See you soon, son."

Gregor° shrugged as Michaels leaned over to show Dane a scroll rendering a map of the new route. Along the edge of the map new threat assessments began listing the numerous dangers that such an open field entailed. Dane began thinking about the codenames of the Creator and other high profiles. Alec's security detail codename appeared on the map as, *'Mastermind'*, and Abby's as, *'Mage'*. He knew Mother's codename was, *'Maker'*, and his own was *'Mark'*.

Too many questions were swarming around Dane's mind. Before he could get a handle of the situation, the group had reached their destination. Abby was the first to greet Dane when exiting the security SDV. Her codename appeared as a marker over her head before Dane shook the Augmented Reality (AR) away. Abby slapped Dane's shoulder before congratulating him.

"I knew he'd call you! Did you get it? You talked right?"

"Kind of but not really – He talked and I listened, you know like usual."

"Well, I was about to ask him when he asked me for a direct line to you. I was a little surprised at the request, but now you're here! Is something wrong?"

More AR warnings of potential dangers appeared across Dane's vision. The blinking markers only served to clutter his thinking before a soft wind reminded him of all of the serene nature around them. It provided the needed distraction to offer a kind tone to his sister.

"Yeah, I'm here. We're here, the whole team now. Are there any security measures underway that you're aware of, because the guys just seem to be lingering about."

Michaels stepped to lean in towards Dane and say: "I'm going to take a position now- "

"Don't even worry about it. Nobody cares that we're here, and I really mean nobody – so, stand down."

"Sir, if someone…"

Michaels received a dead stare from Dane. Abby began to slowly distance herself as another security team member closed in. Former Enforcer, N-12 offered a half salute before welcoming Dane and Michaels.

"Well alright, the boss is in! – and Dane's here too!"

Dane took in another deep breath before noticing two men near running towards the Creator. In pushing past N-12, Dane ordered of the two: "Hey! Stop right there!"

The men only slowed their pace. They appeared more confused than threatened. Abby stepped in Dane's line of sight to reassure the men that all was well with a big smile and a waving motion. Alec offered nothing more than a smirk.

Abby turned towards Dane too but only to roll her eyes in disbelief. With a tempered voice she urged Dane to recognize what she assumed he should have already known: "Those are Elites! They're a large part of the reason we're here. Please review the itinerary because these are sensitive issues that require diplomacy and trust. The last thing these businessmen need is doubt."

"Alright I got it. We'll stand down – now even more than before, thanks."

Abby smiled at Dane's kind attempt to spare her from the storm brewing inside of him. She hurried to catch up to the Creator who had already started walking a few yards ahead. For Abby, who was spending less time than ever with Dane, it was not common for him to be as furious as he appeared to be and for that matter, equally as capable of taming such sentiment.

Behind Dane, a family, most likely tourists, was riding a tandem bicycle car. They rang their bicycle bell to warn Dane of their presence. Dane flinched at the sound and placed a hand over his sidearm but did not draw the weapon. The entire team was scattered about him, waiting on his command. Michaels filled the void by ordering part of the team to follow after Abby, the Creator, and the fellow Elites.

Dane kept to staring at the grass along the path before green lighting Michaels and Hunter°. Gregor° nudged Dane and warned: "We should get going, before they lose us."

The two headed towards the Creator's general direction. Dane could not help but notice all of the families enjoying their day. He wondered how many of them were human, Andi, or mixed families. He figured it really did not matter either way – his role was to be a follower and that was all he was ever meant to be. The idea drilled itself further with every step. All of the rhetoric in the news and online about Andis being nothing more than robotic copies of *real* humans began playing out before his very eyes. The notion was then juxtaposed against Alec near begging Dane to live for his own dreams and to stop following others'. Yet here he was dragging his feet step after step in order to shadow a *real* human.

Dane's drifting in thought alarmed Gregor°. "If something's still troubling you, how's about a drink?"

"No, I'm supposed to be working – no, you know what, yeah, give me a drink."

Gregor°'s cooled compartment opened to reveal an ice cold drink. Dane took a good long drink and chucked the can into a trash bin. A nearby service ID dropped his broom at the insolence of not placing the can in the proper receptacle. Dane did not bother to correct the error. Instead, he moved on.

When having caught up to the group, Dane stood among his security team as Alec did among the Elites. For a moment, the two took note of the other – Alec was about to acknowledge his son, but Dane had turned away.

Feeling brave and rather curious in the moment, Dane ordered Michaels to listen in to the Creator's conversation regardless of the legality of doing so. It was a fine line between family business and public roles. Michaels slid a folding visor over his face to grimace before Hunter° began transferring audio directly to Dane's MIMs. Dane peeked at Alec before placing a pair of sunglasses on.

After a hiccup of audio feedback the sound came in over Dane's MIMs. One of the two men was speaking: "...the investors are set and the missing Elites have rendered a dividing partial lead regarding control of their base. It's a complex attempt your encircling, Alec – they'll be frozen out."

"I have what I want with your support. Everything is in order and there is nothing they can do to undo the quagmire they've fallen into. We only asked that they contribute to their own demise. What more could they possibly ask for with the options they have left. They wished death upon me when I offered a floating favor."

"Look Alec, he's right! With all of us on board, the European partners will freeze out any remaining Elites. It was horrible enough that they had to go under in hiding and maneuver about like- "

"They've been late in understanding what was happening. I'm not going to start having a conscience for their choice, remember *their* choice! – this business gives and takes, you're both well aware of this. These lost souls are on the run and the door is already closed."

"Exactly as you planned, Alec? I'm glad I'm on your side. There were signs abound while the divide increased. I agree in that they had ample time to move, but chose instead to take their money and run... run themselves in circles and pretty much into oblivion. All is well underway on my end."

"On mine too, Alec – as it was always meant to be, huh? Thank you for meeting with us before you know, it's all official."

"Of course. Say hello to you family for me, the both of you. Times have changed since I last saw any of them. And, as for family time, did you know that my son's with me today? He's right over..."

Dane quickly snapped his MIMs off and laughed at nothing in particular. His teammates became confused but caught on and laughed in speculative support. Before Dane knew it Alec had tapped him on the arm to say: "Walk with me, son – team, we're heading back on the road!"

The security detail began to fall in after the two started along the manicured property grounds. They were given a wide berth for such moments were uncommon. Alec began with an open question: "Are you doing better now?"

Dane couldn't believe the nerve of such a man. It was as if it were all a game. Dane would do his best to try and play along.

"You see me wearing a monkey suit, no? I mean where else can I pretend to be doing something for nothing – you don't take your own security serious, why should anyone else, right?"

"I do take security serious. If you've noticed we're in good company, in the safety of friends. People here are free to live, look for yourself at how happy everyone is."

"Why are you meeting with business people in plain sight and with no planning for your security? I don't know who orders my team to stand down more often, me or you? And I'm not as confident in all of the *friendliness* around here as you are. The *people* could be dangerous."

At that very moment a child eating his gelato took notice of Dane's scolding tone before moving on. Dane sighed and planted the palm of his hand over his face.

"Are we doing this again, Dad? You say you want me to learn yet you head off to another secret but very public location to conduct confidential business with connections I most likely will never see again. And please tell me what I'm supposed to learn from the experience?"

"You're correct, and with reason. The world… is changing. I know because I'm part of the old order – and I'll tell you what, it isn't welcome to change. It's holding on with everything it has. I want you at my side so you can see, witness even, what's occurring."

"So I'm to stop and smell the roses so to speak? In what world is that learning or even being by your side? Yes, you can say I haven't tagged along, but it's the same thing every time. Rushing to go nowhere, that's the message I'm left with."

After a few steps in silence Alec changed course cutting through the grass. Dane followed along without question. Alec continued: "Sometimes a leader must act without consent. Not because of wanting to or having to either. When choices that affect many are made, they are done so with care, with research, and a certain amount of calculation based on information not known to all. Trust in such leaders offers progress towards a goal. Those goals must benefit as many as possible – for that is the trust we are working on behalf of."

Before Dane had noticed, the two were already alongside the convoy of security SDVs. The shortcut saved time and limited Alec's exposure to the public. Alec waved the team to standby so he could finish his thought: "Dane, I want you to be able to do anything you want. The world is being made over as we speak so that you and your siblings can experience a new world – one of order and a peaceful existence. Your world will be shared, you show me what the future has in store every time I see you."

Dane removed his sunglasses and said: "There's more to life than being your shadow. I think you want me to be on vacation like how you feel when you're dealing with your friends – I don't think anything makes you feel as happy as when you get what you wanted. I've heard you tell people that we're, you know your children, are the best thing in the world. Look at me, I'm not free of interested in the lines you drop to make people smile after meeting with them."

"Here's the thing, son. It's taken a long time, in fact longer than you've been born, to be, to have positioned myself where I am today. These people are not my friends, they are my competition, my enemies. What you interpret as small talk is a dance of verbal victory – one where I remind them of how horribly wrong they were to cross me, how wondrous it is to have beaten them, and then a final reminder of who we were fighting for. We meet in public because they don't want to lose more face than they already have. All of these years have not been for nothing, the shift in power has been our making and responsibility. We are the strongest, so we suffer the most to ease others' lives - that is true leadership. You may feel disconnected from me but believe me, the life you have, the one you lead, has a cost – no, don't you turn away from me! It has a cost, there is a price, one that involves power to achieve order, one that allows the future to progress without the anchors of discontents keeping good people such as yourself from being free to live a peaceful life. The old order's poisonous drive was to drain the life out of its citizenry, you and your siblings will have the best opportunity to give back like never before in history. Trust that it will work, because that's all that really matter."

Dane remained unconvinced. As Alec waited for a response, Dane became rigid in posture before leaving towards the lead SDV of the convoy. For Dane, the job of watching the Creator vacationing was to continue. As for where the next meeting would take place or for what reason, it mattered little to Dane – he deleted the itinerary as soon as it appeared on his armored truck's screen.

14 HEMORRHAGING

Though a press briefing would soon begin at Fort William in India, the Helena Administration's Press Secretary, Abigail Helena, had not yet adjusted to her new role. Having been groomed for the position by Mother's Shades of Infinite Order (SIOs), she welcomed the opportunity to represent the family. But so many issues were surfacing with every bold step taken by the recently elected Helena Administration, many occurring simultaneously, that Abby's original plan to hold weekly briefings instead of daily frequently lagged.

The subject of this press briefing was to serve more as a formal gesture of transparency relating to the latest acquired countries than one of procedural necessity. Abby arrived to the briefing immaculately dressed and ready to navigate the scrutiny. "Good afternoon ladies and gentlemen, thank you for being here today. Let me begin by saying that, we in the Helena Administration have been so graciously welcomed by the citizens of this majestic state. You have gone above and beyond in your courtesy and openness in becoming part of the United States of America. Your continued success is assured, for we are here to help build all citizens. My father has always held India in high regard and is honored to have it strengthen our union. Let's begin with questions, from the front here… yes, go ahead."

A local reporter asked: "Does the Helena family have any regard for maintaining the identity of a people that have existed for thousands of years? Or does your family plan to eradicate such a past?"

Abby had been asked similar questions about the processing of citizens from the country that had been known as Mexico. She answered: "What we are doing and have done elsewhere in the preservation of a culture is to free the citizenry from the propagation of archaic lines of thinking. Our citizens are free to believe what they choose. If citizens want to keep their culture, they are more than free to do so, as long as they are not breaking any laws or infringing on the liberties of others. We promote collaborative integration above all else. We offer are elevated living conditions that stress opportunity and guarantee access to services for all."

Abby motioned for the next question. A second reporter asked: "It has been reported that in a southern state of America - the Yucatan, in particular - Andi-free zones have been established for human populations that do not want anything to do with your proposed new world. Are citizens free to live within such a sovereign state? Will such a territory be set aside for the people of India who do not want to fall under your family's rule?"

Abby answered: "It is true that such an area has been set aside for some of our most ardent of citizens. Such freedoms are tantamount for all citizens living within the United States. In fact, we are planning for another such territory. As for the case in the Yucatan - we allowed for their leadership to have options on requirements to ensure their population's welfare. Any future establishment of a sovereign nation within the country will be made public upon approval by congress..."

The reporter interrupted: "If such allocations or their negotiations are held in private, how will the public know if these territories are truly free of Andi control?"

Abby continued: "Decisions on privacy will fall on the party initiating the request. For example, it was up to the local farmers union of the Yucatan whether such negotiations were made public. Look, we are not going out of our way to set up such freedoms only to sabotage them with intrusive oversight. The fact of the matter is, because these territories are within our domain, they must be protected *and* respected."

Another reporter asked: "What does the Helena Administration plan to do about sectarianism and other long standing divisions within ethnic groups in countries throughout the Middle East or Sub-Saharan Africa? The actions that have taken place have not stabilized the region as was previously guaranteed."

The reporter's tone agitated Abby. "The United States has ramped up all construction throughout our Middle Eastern and Sub-Saharan States. We have a history of peaceful order and progress there. Think of our newest states in the Levant as prime examples. In Israel and Palestine, we have worked extensively to promote the welfare of both states. Of course some residual issues persist, but let us be clear on this, the two states are at peace and their success in relation to threats and all criminal activity are at record lows. Some tensions are flaring within some of the newer provinces that have yet to be fully integrated, and not all territories have been brought up to speed. But regardless of these few cases, the process is moving ahead. Creating new states was never meant to be an easy task. If it were, then it would have taken place long ago. Our presence has made tremendous strides relative to Arab-Israeli relations. In fact the borders between the two states are completely open. We have provided overwhelming support and opportunities for families to flourish. With abundant education and opportunity, their standard of living has grown exponentially. They are neighbors living in prosperity."

A reporter quickly asked: "Does your family now control the drug trade?"

"Drug abuse had been a problem. Our medical techniques have been readily available for drug abusers that want to be free of their addiction. The best part has been its cost, none whatsoever. We legalized all drugs while successfully taking over all supply lines and systems that were previously maintained by the cartels. Legality has killed the stigma, the cost, and the shame."

A reporter from China asked: "Why has the expansion of the American Empire come to a halt? Has the line in the sand been drawn due to the enforcement and consolidation of the renewed Sino Russian Alliance, and are we currently experiencing a Second Cold War due to American forces being spread too thin around the globe? Should the administration have reached out to its past top economic partner during their most recent crises instead of capitalizing on their misfortune?"

The wave of questions unsettled Abby. She had been kept out of the loop regarding plans for China and Russia. The revolution that wrecked China's economy took place long before her father had begun his campaign. The Sino Russian Alliance was a nonstarter within the family, so she deflected the question as best she could.

"There have been plenty of developments that have occurred over the last month. The amount of sensitive materials and developments under way is not something that can be easily shared. As for being spread too thin, we have no deadlines on any expansion or strengthening of our interests that have not been made public. Negotiations with the European Alliance continue to improve, while the Israeli and Palestinian ties strengthen every week. In the Americas, our new states are under construction. We worked extensively to bind our ties with China in the years after their revolution. Unfortunately, discourse between our respective countries has ceased since their division. We have all faced this difficult time in our own manner. As for as their alliance with Russia is concerned, we know that it is a relationship of necessity. We have no standing in dictating what other countries should do... Thank you."

The vagueness of Abby's responses created more questions than they answered. The briefing had pushed orchestrated narratives to their limits. After the briefing she met with Zach, Teddy°, and her own ID, Mari°. They had been watching her from behind the backdrop blue curtain. Zach placed his arm around her as she vented: "What was that!"

The two walked with their IDs towards a small fort in a restricted area. Abby remained silent until they entered its hall. Then she slapped her notes against her palm. "It's ridiculous! I'm kept out of the loop. How am I'm supposed to defend classified information?"

Abby, Zach, and their IDs entered a wide conference room, one recently remodeled to Abby's liking. At its center was a large square of plush couches highlighted by expensive furnishings.

Zach had attended the press briefing to check on Mari°'s recovery, and to observe the firsthand rebuilding of India. He could not resist the opportunity to gain access to Indian military technology. Teddy° had snuck a few small pieces of that technology into a hidden compartment along his thorax.

Despite inevitable setbacks the United States remained the wealthiest country the world had ever known. Abby's father had nearly received every Electoral College vote in the previous month to win a landslide victory and assume control. Even before the election cycle had run its course, most of the world had fallen under Andi rule. So much had changed within such a short period of time that it seemed impossible to keep up. Reports would pour into Abby's office at such an impossible rate that she welcomed any help Zach and the IDs could offer. And though the Shades worked on policies, she was the administration's voice. They worked tirelessly to see that demands were met like clockwork, yet Abby often felt behind.

The Middle East had been united due to Eric's involvement and the implementation of several key economic and political reforms. Political lines were redrawn to support the new states, with each state designated for different sects and ethnic groups. Most of Africa's countries had gained statehood, their standards of living now nearly to that of the rest of the union. Ophelia had been welcomed throughout the new Central American States, but Brazil and other neighboring countries were holding out.

Abby's burden was to convince humanity that it was in its best interests to step aside so that the Andi could provide them with a higher standard of living. Without offending them, she had to tell them they had failed. The main problem she had was keeping power out of human hands. The plans for each of the acquired territories were designed to stave off corruption, which required keeping power out of human hands – the main problem Abby faced. In the eyes of the Andi, humans had a near obsession with taking advantage of others they perceived as potential threats was at the heart of the problem. Keeping humans from wanting to gain more power became an issue itself. Because the Andi were aware the allure of corruption arose whenever a ruling party gained too much power, they placed integrity at the foundation of their governance. Also because each country had its own set of moral laws relating to what individuals were allowed to engage in, there was the notion of secured freedoms to consider.

For generations the majority of the world had lived in poverty. To provide opportunities for all was at first glance an impossible responsibility, but it was one of the focal points of the transition. Humans had to adapt to the reality that living for the sake of wealth was removed. Relinquishing the tendency to want more had to slowly enter the collective mindset. In time, humans would be freed from having to actively sustain a livelihood. The changes were designed to create a more balanced life, with a higher state of being possible, but it had to be earned.

Abby looked at Zach as a buffer. And even though he was well intentioned, he was often unconcerned, and his focus often proved self-serving. He was happiest when collecting more materials to add to his personal collections. Abby, too, was not free of such thinking. Her status had given her a confidence that demanded extravagance. Zach framed her as such. Whenever he observed her talking about her professional outlook, she often let elitist terms like *blue collar* or *bourgeois* slip out. Both thought the other was too concentrated with satisfying future desires and not concerned enough with current necessities, so the issue of want versus need often arose, resulting in charges made against one another.

Just as they began to relax, the conference room doors slid open, but no one entered. They had hoped to see Eric or Jacob. Abby called out: "Eric, is that you?" When no answer came, Abby figured it was Jacob. "I know it's you. You can come out now, we won't bite."

The group began to feel unnerved as something kept the doors open.. Zach tried to keep his imagination from running away as Teddy° crawled behind one of the couches. A terrible thought had taken hold of the ID. The items he was storing must have been reported missing. He considered hiding his stash under the couch. Finally, Zach gathered enough courage to say: "Jacob, it has to be you. The only other person that it could be is Eric. We're in a heavily fortified base surrounded by an army of drones!"

Abby had had enough. She called to the screen wall: "Call, Eric." The screen wall initiated the connection, bringing Jacob rushing into the room to cancel the call. "Are you crazy?"

Abby mocked him. "Did I just scare a ghost back to life?"

"Touché. I'm curious, was that a tactical move or were you crying out for big brother?"

Abby took a sip of her wine. "Of course it was tactical. Who do you think I am? Zach."

She cackled and they looked at Zach. He was still recovering his nerve. Teddy°'s eyes peered over the back of the couch. He quietly refilled his secret compartment. Mari° flew over to a mirror and stretched her wings as Jacob walked over to pat Zach's shoulder and to kiss Abby on the cheek before sitting down. His wasp ID Fitz° flew over to the back of the couch where Teddy° was still crouched and was met with a white mustached smile.

Jacob wriggled into the plush upholstery, trying to get comfortable. "So what was the drama before a ghost mysteriously interrupted you two?" he asked.

Abby responded: "Did you know that for most of humanity's history, more than ninety percent of the population has lived in misery? It's a good thing the Andi came along. Most Andis serve for the betterment of society. Why is that so hard for them to understand? I don't know how they survived all this time. Our duty as lead Andis is not one we chose for ourselves. It hasn't been easy."

Jacob looked at Zach. "Do you feel the same or is it only fancy pants here?"

Zach rolled his eyes in jest. "I can't complain. My comforts are met. I do believe humankind is indebted to us. We take care of them whether they like it or not. To ease their fears, Abby has to present everything as more pleasant than what it is. You can't tell them life is complicated. Humans want to be coddled, but would never admit it. Their pride is too strong and resolve too stubborn."

Teddy° moaned an amen.

Jacob struggled to respond: "I totally disagree with you! Your remarks about the welfare of humanity are oversimplified. People don't take advantage of others because it's in their nature to do so. They do so because at some time in their life they learned to. I've learned to support growth and not criticize faults. Look at the examples you chose to make your argument. We're not helping solely for their sake. We all have to live together."

Fitz° looked Teddy° over as Jacob continued: "Earlier, you mentioned the humans living off the grid. The truth is, they're being herded onto those reservations. We promised them equality for their lands and then we forced them onto reservations of our choosing. With their wealth having no real value, there isn't much they can do about it. We write our own history. This is the problem with your position. You have to siphon an incredible amount of history in real time. Your argument is catalogued for future hearts and minds to review in hindsight." Jacob paused to looked at the dirt on his hands. "For me, the struggle has been between truth and duty. If Eric tells me to jump off a bridge, I jump. If he tells me to end a life, I end it. That is the world in which I operate and I'm thankful to the Creator for allowing me to serve. I've lived through some things I thought I wouldn't survive. When I hear you say that the humans are only charity cases, or that Andis and drones exist to serve *us*, I take a step back. My duty has to override the truth. I don't have the luxury of deciphering its perception. People, Andis, and drones have paid with *their* lives in serving our country and *your* truth."

Abby had begun reviewing her shopping cart on a pen scroll. She remembered needing to change her clothing order, only half listening as Jacob spoke. She checked her discount with the sale price on the scroll, convincing herself that he wouldn't mind she would tune in and catch up. But Jacob took note of her distraction. "The SRA isn't concerned with Super Taco Tuesday."

Abby made eye contact and nodded. "Yeah, I think so too. Yes, you are right." Checking back into the conversation, she asked: "Why is my father not integrating the SRA to create more wealth?"

"I'm not in a position to have an opinion on what your father wants." Jacob stood and kissed Abby goodbye as his radio crackled with Eric's voice. "Jacob, get to the tarmac." He answered: "On my way, Sir."

Jacob and Fitz° waved goodbye. Abby turned to Zach. "You're so easy to win over."

"I'm too easy to win over? He didn't kiss me goodbye."

She smiled and said: "Regardless of how much Jacob loves me, he's too close to the problem to see the bigger picture. His status limits his vision. But if that status were to say one day be at my side, well… that would be a different story."

15 TOAST OF THE TOWN

Meadows blurred along the roadside as Alec gazed out of his limo's window at Venice. An anniversary celebration for former members of the European Union entering the American Union was to occur and it would coincide with the year's Mardi Gras festivities. Alec could think of no better place to celebrate. Negotiations had been intense but well worth the struggle. The more Alec had pressed the higher demands had soared. In the end, it was the workforce that shifted the balance as more examples of higher standards of living for new members to the American Union became known. With the realization taking hold, there was no turning back.

Days had passed since the ceremonial signing of the union in Florence, Italy. The media showcased Alec as he signed alongside Abby. Dane was nearly out of frame, and only appeared in some of the variant images.

Alec's attention returned to the empty interior of the

limousine. He was wearing a costumed black robe and had a white mask with gold laced designs on the seat next to him. His thoughts centered on Dane as he ordered the convoy to stop. Alec used the limo's com system to get a hold of the lead vehicle. "Dane, I want to talk to you."

Dane responded: "On my way." He exchanged nods with Michaels and after patting Gregor°, stepped out of the armored truck and walked to the limo. Alec welcomed him. "Come in, have a seat. Want something to drink?"

Dane slid his father's mask away as he took a seat in the limo. "No thanks," he said.

Alec and his ID Billy° raised their highball glasses. Billy° took his leave and returned to watching the road from the now sealed off driving cab. Alec tried to appeal to Dane. "Look, I know you're not too happy with your assignment. I get it. What concerns me though, is if you understand why."

The comment hit a nerve. "I guess I don't. I'm too dense. You drag me and my team around to keep us out of trouble to serve as doormen or repairmen. I get that much. We observe you living and have nothing to report!"

Mildly annoyed, Alec continue: "I wanted you with me so you could learn a thing or two. I kept hoping to spark the curiosity I know you have. How many times have I called for you? I don't want to get upset about what could have been - it's not my style, and it isn't yours either."

Dane did not appreciate the multiple insults. "There's not supposed to be any sacrifice in doing what you want. During indoctrination we were told we could do whatever we want. I wanted to be an Enforcer. Now I'm in a monkey suit."

Alec stared into his empty glass. "To understand the present, you have to learn about the past. After you settled on the military you continued chasing dreams for years. The war was over before you came around. You couldn't stand it. You can't live other's dreams. Your generation took for granted the humiliating cross carried by those who came before you. Life's rarely as you expect it to be. At best, life is absurd. The sooner you accept that, the sooner you can adapt and overcome obstacles."

Dane's eyes glared with frustration. "I don't understand you. If you know me better than I know myself, then tell me what I'm doing here. What's all of this for? I'm not happy and you know this. I don't want to learn just to settle for things as they are."

Alec attempted to reason with Dane: "That's not what I want for you. I want you to open your eyes. You can begin by admitting you know nothing. The world is as large or as small as you make it. We've traveled the world, but you've never taken the time to look outside your own. Read, live, and accept things are beyond your control. In dismissing reality you've stunted your growth and imprisoned your mind."

Alec stopped himself. He looked at Dane in silence as the limousine drove on. Dane's thoughts were processing the points made, but he could not find it within himself to challenge his father. With furrowed brows, Dane ignored the gleaming waters beneath the bridge road to Venice.

After a hard gulp, Alec continued: "Tonight is special. After a few private parties, I want you to join me in celebrating. How does that sound?"

Dane appreciated his father's sincerity. "Can't we just have some fun tonight?"

Alec smiled widely. "That's entirely up to you. There are plenty of Venetian masks for you and your team."

The parking lot at the end of the roadway was congested, so the convoy stopped along a row of tourist SDVs and city buses. The occupants of the convoy exited their vehicles as tourists bustled along. Alec donned his mask, as masks and robes were distributed to Drones and IDs draped in burlap. They moved along walkways and over small bridges to reach their private convoy of water transports. During the next hours, they cycled through many private parties, some so private they required verbal passwords. After the first few hotels and villas, Dane became agitated with the routine. He directed his anger towards Michaels, ordering him to relax. Michaels nodded in responding: "Yes, Sir."

At one of the larger villas, Dane stepped back to view the enormity of the room. He saw his father meeting someone with an entourage. Checking his scroll he noticed that the TECO cameras had gone offline, but their lights were still on. Only Mother or Nero would do such a thing. A Shade dressed in grey robes and hood touched Dane's shoulder, startling him. With a haunting voice she assured him: "The Creator is with Spirit."

Dane felt at ease for the moment. The room was filled with what he could only assume were Shades. He tried to guess which one was Mother. Alec finally revealed her location by giving her a kiss. Oddly, they did so with their masks on. Then Mother took hers off and Alec followed suit. Dane switched his scroll to audio eavesdropping to listen to their conversation. He heard his father's voice through the crowd.

"Do we ever take our masks off?"

Mother responded: "How many masks are there?"

Alec took a drink. "We are all each other's dreams and nightmares."

The connection faded but then returned. Mother's voice echoed: "... Abby and Zach are with me. She is looking for Dane. If only the rest of the Helena children were not so busy."

Dane saw Alec lean his head back as Abby made a small commotion, moving everyone aside to hug the Creator. "You should have seen it, I scared the life out of Michaels! I can't find Dane anywhere. Are we *all* supposed to go to the Piazza San Marco?"

Alec answered: "I'm heading there later. There's going to be fireworks tonight. I haven't been there for some time. The festivities give me the opportunity to do so."

Abby smiled. "Well, I'd love to go, but I was there all morning with my friends. We want to stay here tonight, it's a great view. Plus, we'll be away from the crowds."

Abby interrupted as Alec was about to speak: "It's ok. Oh, my friends are waving to me from the hall. See you later!" She kissed him, and bid everyone a quick goodbye.

Mother turned her gaze in Dane's direction as she addressed Alec. "Your understanding is admirable, Creator." All the Shades in the room bowed to create a clearing for Alec to locate Dane. Dane, seeing his father, un-cupped his ear and smiled. He noticed that evening was near as Mother bid Alec farewell and a Shade handed him back his mask.

Alec walked the clearing towards Dane. The two met outside with the rest of the team and boarded their water transports. No one spoke during the choppy ride over to the piazza. Looking out at the walkways as they passed, Dane thought he saw Tavy. But she disappeared within a group so fast that he wasn't sure if it really was her. He shook his head in disbelief.

Evening had set as the group spread out across the historic Piazza San Marco. Michaels was again ordered to stand down. He moved out to an unobstructed niche between pillars and leaned against Hunter°. Gregor° waddled along with Dane, admiring costumes and the festivities. Dane had managed to load his compartments full of drinks. It was the least he could do to make the evening tolerable. Alec's Billy° remained on the waterfront, captivated by the water splashing over the stony shore.

After a few hours gallivanting, Dane met up with his father. He wanted to be relieved of duty regardless of having done nothing. Alec had been drinking throughout the evening, and finally seeing Dane again, hugged him tight and offered a hearty hello. Dane had also been drinking and couldn't help laughing a little. He was first to speak: "So I guess you have to be liquored-up to cozy up to me. Are we done here or are we going to keep drinking with strangers?"

Alec countered: "I'm glad you're comfortable enough to talk with me."

A black helicopter zoomed overhead. It hovered, then moved toward the waterway at the mouth of the piazza.

Several costumed attendees cleared a place as a group rappelled to the ground. The group consisted of two officers, a team of ICs, a wasp ID, and a bioluminescent scorpion. Dane's team stumbled over out of sheer curiosity.

Nero and his team ignored the group as the helicopter moved out. Alec was happy to see him. But Nero was in no mood to be pleasant. As he was about to salute, Alec gave him a hug. "Welcome! Thank goodness you're here."

Nero's anger turned to confusion at the uncharacteristic public display of affection. "Um, thank you, Father. I'm… concerned about your security. I've sent for more security but was only permitted a team. They are to stay at the border by your authority. This open piazza is not safe. We have to get you out of here. There are reports of possible…"

Alec laughed, still holding onto Nero. "I'm not leaving. We're having a great time. I don't remember a thing, but that's alright!"

Nero turned towards Dane as Gregor° retreated into his body. "What do you think you're doing? Why can't you answer my calls? Are *all* your communications offline? I'm surprised you even have a team on the rooftops!"

Dane shifted his stance forward. "I don't have anyone on the rooftops…"

Nero's eyes widened as he yelled an order as loud as he could: "Up!"

A cloaked man had cut the guard wires from the campanile bell tower across the waterway, and now fired his sniper rifle at the masked man who hugged the Director of National Intelligence. Of all the masked attendees, only one would have been allowed such familiarity. The shot tore through Dane's shoulder as he stepped toward Nero. The bullet shattered Dane's shoulder, deflecting away from Alec. It knocked them both to the ground.

Michaels caught his Palm Special Sniper Rifle in midair as Hunter° ejected it, and then launched smoke canisters in the general direction of the sniper shot. The ID also popped a mini dragonfly drone scout. The mini drone began highlighting all movement and immediately calculated the sniper's position. Michaels and Hunter° ran towards Dane. The mini drone scoped the bell tower across the waterway for Michaels. The sniper was preparing to take another shot as Alec struggled to move under Dane's weight. A wall of smoke began to rise. Through the commotion, Gregor° stood and provided cover for both Dane and the Creator. A second and third shot hit Gregor° as the sniper tried to get him out of the way. Though the ID had strengthened his forward light shields the shot still punished his defenses. A fourth shot hit the shield before Michaels had a clear line of sight. Then, with one shot, Michaels took the sniper's head clear off.

Suddenly rockets were fired from a boat idling in the waterway. Dane's entire team and half of Nero's ICs were obliterated. Nero's men had set their shields, but a second too late. Their helicopter was blown out of the sky as it returned. As Dane rose to his feet, he witnessed his team's fate. Nero, who had been closest in proximity to the fallen ICs, was riddled with shrapnel by the blast, which sent his body scrapping across the ground to a stop. In response, Michaels unloaded on the boat with precision kills.

The survivors of the initial attacks created a perimeter to protect the Creator. Molotov cocktails began to rain down from the rooftops without pause. Hordes of surrounding attendees were ready to move in and finish them off. Without hesitation, Jordan ordered his ID Kurtz° and the remaining ICs to fire at will. The number of bodies falling was disproportionate to the amount of fire that continued to pour from the IDs and ICs. Nearly every shot ended a life. Wildly blinking blips flashed from Hunter°'s mini drone as it relayed enemy markers to Jordan and his team.

The inner defense perimeter concentrated their fire on the rooftops as the firebombing continued. Dane had emptied his rifle and placed his sidearm on the ground, trying his best to cover his father's body and protect it from the fire. Seeing his father's flesh melting away sent him into a panic. Alec was in so much pain. Gregor° attempted to provide extra cover. He had already taken a tremendous amount of damage and was using all his remaining power to recycle his shield's integrity. Hunter° bulldozed over incoming attackers that were attempting to break through the lines of defense. Kurtz° and the ICs continued to unload firepower into the crowds. Nero's RJ° went on a rampage, gouging body after body with its tail. During its killing frenzy it deflected incoming fire and snapped limbs with its large claws.

The team was completely surrounded, their numbers were rapidly dwindling. The heavy bombardment weakened their shielding and skin integrity as small arms fire began to drop several of the ICs. The waves of people attacking them seemed to have no end.

As their inner defenses were finally breached, IC attack helicopters arrived. They lit the rooftops with firepower as mini drones touched down across the grounds and rooftops. The attackers were mowed down as they attempted to scatter. Jordan ordered that the remaining stragglers be captured alive. Other interceptor transports pursued any and all movement across the waterways. In particular, they hovered over the place where the initial shot was fired. Drones were dropped at the Church of San Giorgio Maggiore and at the Cini Foundation. Jordan had taken command, and now orchestrated a thorough search and investigation of the area.

Nero peeled his eyes open with his remaining arm. He managed to hoist himself on top of a couple of bodies as the firefight came to a close. Unable to locate his rifle or sidearm, his gaze fell to his legs that remained on fire. The attack had left him with broken legs, a missing arm, clouded vision, and muffled hearing. His face, though he was not aware of it yet, was pocked with pieces of shrapnel. When the smoke cleared, Nero could see Dane holding onto a charred body. Nero tried calling out to them, but everything sounded as if it were underwater.

Dane looked upon his father's horribly burned face. The Creator's flesh was fuming. In despair, Dane pleaded: "Please don't die. Please don't die. I can't... Gregor°'s got first aid with nano, just hold on."

Alec's eyes searched the space between them before focusing on his son. "Dane... tell every... I love them."

First aid was administered, but provided only minor comfort. The burns were too severe. Jordan extinguished the embers still glowing on Nero's legs as RJ° restored his vision and hearing. Nero continued gazing in agony at his father.

Alec had an odd expression on his face and began talking as if to the stars overhead. He reached out, and began to mumble. As the remaining color drained from his face, Dane held tightly to him, pressing their foreheads together.

As Jordan helped him sit upright, Nero called out. Catching sight of his father's fractured mask, Nero wept as he slipped into unconsciousness.

16 EPILOGUE

On the night of the Creator's assassination, Eric Helena had been going over several of the last countries not under Andi influence or control. The greater areas served as buffer countries to the SRA. Nighttime global scans showed the areas as dark and with little activity. There were swaths of territories in need of key military positions to build on. The Creator had insisted on Eric's researching the areas regardless of the static situation of moving against the SRA. An ad hoc camp had been set up along the western outskirts of the Sahara Desert.

Several of Eric's teams were hard at work throughout the night when Eric's second in command, Jacob had been directly contacted by Nero's second, Jordan. It was unusual for Jacob to receive any contact from his twin brother so when the call came in on a secure line Jacob set everything aside to listen to what he had to say.

"Go ahead, Jordan - what is it?."

After a minor pause, Jordan spoke: "A crime has been

committed against our Creator, and he is no longer alive. We are doing everything we can to get to the bottom of this horrific act. Please note we did all that we could – Nero has also been severely injured. Please let the Supreme Commander know what has occurred. That is all for now."

And with that, the call was ended.

Jacob swallowed hard. Several thoughts flooded his thinking. The one overall difficulty would be in telling Eric. Jacob had no idea how the Supreme Commander would take such news. As immediately as Jacob thought of Jordan not having sent the report on the matter, his ID Fitz° received it. Not wanting to waste time and feeling the immediacy of the situation looming, Jacob needed to share what was known so he headed towards Eric.

Others in the group surrounding Eric took note of Jacob's anxious appearance and awkward hesitation of movement. The high ranking officers respected their commanders' privacy and instead of lingering about they chose to move away. When Eric turned around Jacob motioned for the remaining officers to leave them and they did. The two walked but a few feet towards the already bright morning sky. Eric breathed deep in preparing himself for the bad news.

Jacob searched the floor but said without hesitation: "Sir, I don't know how else to say this so I'll be straight with it. The Creator has been assassinated. He... was- "

Jacob could bring himself to say anything more. It pained him to tell Eric of the Creator's death. Eric motioned as though to say he had heard enough. In partially turning from Jacob, Eric stopped. Unexpected to Jacob, Eric issued an order: "Get ready to go to Kashmir. We have a war to prepare for."

Jacob snapped a salute before being dismissed. Eric was left alone with his thoughts overlooking the shifting dunes.

As soon as the assassination of Alec Helena was complete, news secretly began to travel up the chain of conspirators. At the first eye-witness confirmation of Mr. Helena's emulation, its low level member was killed off. As time passed most loose ends were immediately pruned. It had been advised ahead of time that the cleverness of doing so would keep the ever curious natures of Andi investigators with nothing to go on. They would have nothing more to investigate than literal dead ends. As for electronic paper trails, an extra amount of self-discipline had to be exercised at every level of the conspiracy.

The hedging of such a gambling act was upon the minds of those at every level of the coordinated attack. One of the mid-level men responsible for the crime began allowing doubt to creep into his already tormented existence. He did everything possible to keep off of any electronic devices and to limit his exposure to the regular circles of usual suspects. Not knowing who to trust anymore he finally built up the courage to reach out to his only contact, the contact that hired him to help coordinate the murder of Alec Helena.

The phone rang several times but to no avail. The man inhaled some Sube to take the edge off of his anxiety. After a dizzy spell, the drug's effects left him on the side of the road. He redialed using another throw away phone.

"Why in the world would you call? What's wrong with you! And to think, you've called twice."

Not having expected the call to be answered on the first ring the man cleared his throat and combed the side of his head before answering.

"It's...it's me. I needed to talk to you. You didn't pick up the first time so -"

"I cannot believe you are that stupid! How dare you call me. This phone's monitored on my end regardless of where you call me from. There is nothing that excuses this— "

"I had to! I can't take this anymore! Nobody knows nothing of anyone anymore."

"Where are you?"

The man looked around but then thought better of it.

"I'm sorry, but I don't want to tell you, I can't."

"What you don't understand is that you're already a dead man. Everybody that's contacted anyone else has been taken away or killed outright. I didn't pick up the first time you called because I was infuriated by your lack of discipline. You've' given us both a death sentence."

"But you're you! Don't you have protection?"

"They're here already. I've been waiting for them – this was too hot from the get go. I thought Mr. Randle was contracting me but I was wrong. I don't know if I was swindled by the SRA or not. I've also been losing it."

"Who's there? Who's in charge?"

The line fell silent.

"No! Stop, you can't do this to me – I don't know anything!"

After some more whimpering and wrestling movements the phone echoed with dead air. Not sure if there was someone on the line and too scared to hang up the man gripped the phone.

"Hello?"

"..."

"Whoever you are, I'm sorry- "

"You will be."

"Wha- "

"We've tracked your call, your phone model, its retail date and location. We backtracked every piece of the phone your using. Thanks to your call, we know your identity, your family's locations, and your entire personal and professional history. You and your family have had an extensive web of criminal history. So it will be of no surprise to anyone when I tell you that I've taken the liberty of adding several much more devious charges to your name. There are now numerous additional outstanding warrants for your arrest."

Grid units far above the man continued to examine the man and redraw his position over the last number of months. The current imaging brought the man into a slight three dimensional view for everyone in the room to see. The frantic pacing redrew over itself near where the man had fallen over earlier.

"Wait, what do you mean more charges - devious in what way? I hardly had anything to do with what happened! I'm just a go between!"

"Don't worry about that. The record now shows you having no involvement with anything beyond your own *sick* criminal history."

The man was aghast. There would be new charges of a sick nature in his criminal history, one for the record. How would anyone disprove such things? As the gravity of the situation began to usher in a sense of vertigo, the man dropped the phone as a black transport descended along the empty road.

Jordan radioed the transport.

"Petra, I'll leave him to you."

"Commander, I have him in sight. Everybody's ready - He's not going anywhere."

Petra turned to the team of ICs in the transport. They were at the ready with heavy weapons and drones on standby. She gave the green light and ICs began to drop off from the open bay doors. As the ICs landed with weapons drawn and drones and equipment in tow, the man on the lone roadside did not attempt to run away. The fear of being shot on the spot outweighed any dream of escaping. As he stood frozen in disbelief the approaching group of ICs tossed a small device onto the man's chest. It discharged an electrical shock dropping the man immediately to the ground. The ICs loaded the man unto an arriving medical unit ID. After the bulbous shell enclosed to a suddenly unconscious prisoner, the unit lurched back around to head towards the transport. The isolation of the roadside allowed for the entire incident to go unnoticed.

Once the ICs and their prisoner were aboard the

transport Petra double clicked a transmission complete message to Jordan. He did not have much hope in the potential findings of the arrest but did not want to rule out any avenues. The matter was of upmost importance for all Andis and humans alike. Not only had the Creator been murdered in cold blood but Nero had also been seriously wounded. Jordan was moving fast to organize a complete investigation, one Nero would be proud of. For the moment, two more links were soon to be mind-scrapped for any information relating to the assassination. If nothing came of it, at the very least those involved would suffer tremendously for their involvement.

AFTERWORD

Late in 2009 this story lingered as a recurring dream. The following year, I drew a rough outline and left it alone to study storytelling. I continued to edit my outline until February of 2012. Then I patched together all of the whispers I received from the universe and started a manuscript. It was completed in May of 2013. Many edits, endless research, and studying ensued.

During the writing of this novel: I married, traveled abroad, moved to Northern California, and had my first born daughter, Lulu.

Thanks to our friends and family: Alfonso and Consuelo Mendoza, Cipriano and Lourdes Catudan, Alfonso Jr., Angel, Alex, Adan, and Maria Mendoza, Angelli and Sanya Panma, Annabeth Catudan, Noel Catudan, Nelson Catudan, Jackie Pambid, Michele Pambid, Kevin Valenzuela, Jim Hutchinson, Janel Dawood, Kelly Hua; Victoria Maria, Enrique, and Conrad Lemus, Ascary Salas, Paul Gonzalez, Mayra Salas, Erick Otanez, and Don Luis and Francisca "Panchita" Salas; - And an extra special thank you to Bill Bruner.

I hope you enjoyed the story!

Visit us at www.adrianmendoza.net

Have questions, comments, or suggestions -

Find us on Facebook, Twitter, and Goodreads.

Printed in Great
Britain
by Amazon